BLOOD MOON PACK

LEGION OF VIDAR

SERENITY RAYNE

I would love to dedicate this book to my

Emotional Support Muppet.

Without you being there helping me see past the pain and all the negativity surrounding this project I never would have been able to finish.

PROLOGUE

"BOSS . . ." Charlie shuffles back and forth, practically dancing in the doorway of Leviathan's office, the manilla envelope in his hand crinkling slightly. Anxiety rolls off the flight shifter in waves from standing in the Dragon's presence.

Leviathan looks up from the stacks of documents on his desk. His eyes, pools of liquid mercury, lock on the fidgety Raven shifter. Extending his huge hand out, Leviathan uses his telekinesis to rip the envelope from Charlie's hand. It flies across the room and over the desk with ease.

Shocked, Charlie stumbles back, falling against the door-frame. Gasping for air, he stares wide-eyed at his boss and the envelope now in his hands. His eyes blacken just before shifting to his Raven form and taking off.

A deep rumble reverberates within the Wyrm's chest as he shakes his head, watching the Raven depart. Shifting a single digit into a talon, Leviathan slices open the top of the envelope. The ripping of paper echoes in the room as he focuses on getting to the contents within. Flipping the envelope upside down, he dumps the contents onto the desk. Several demographic sheets fall out along with a five-by-seven color photo. Ignoring the paperwork, he picks up the picture and stares at it. A beautiful twenty-something-year-old female stares back at him with the palest blue eyes he's ever seen. It reminds him of his beloved Omega, Celeste.

Platinum-blonde, almost white hair and pale-blue eyes can mean only one thing—a Snow Leopard shifter. "Celeste?" His deep, gravelly voice echoes through the halls of his mansion. He knows his mate heard him. While he waits for her arrival, he turns his focus back to business. He picks up the demographics sent to him with the photograph and reads. She was apparently adopted by the Targus pride in southern Montana shortly after birth.

"Yes, my love?" Celeste's soft soothing voice draws Leviathan from his ruminative thoughts. His eyes lift and drift slowly over his mate's voluptuous form, and he smiles in appreciation.

"What information can you give me about your people? A female Snow Leopard shifter was abducted, and I'll be sending the Blood Moon pack to rescue her." Bone plates shift under the ebony skin on his face as he regards his mate, his protective streak triggered by a female in danger.

Gliding across his office, she stands before him and slightly lowers her eyes. His large hands wrap around her waist, pulling her into his lap. "If there's a feline in that club, send him to speak with her first. Wolves or Bears will frighten her, unless she's an Alpha like you, my love." Her lithe hand rests on his chest as she snuggles into his embrace.

For several heartbeats, he presses his full lips to her temple as he ponders what she said. "She is like you, my treasure. I believe Claws is a Lion. Will he do?" He softens his tone to soothe his mate, lightly nuzzling her cheek affectionately.

"Yes, my love, he will be perfect for that," she purrs in his ear, snuggling in close again before kissing his cheek. Her arms wrap around his neck as she hugs him, pleased with his suggestion.

A rumble emanates from his chest as a smile spreads across his lips. "Would you mind shifting for me, my love? The boys will have an advantage if they can see a Snow Leopard before being sent on their mission, in case she shifts to protect herself." His hand caresses her cheek, turning her to face him before kissing her passionately.

"Anything your heart desires, my love." Celeste purrs, returning the kiss. She slides off his lap and shifts gracefully into her large, furry Snow Leopard. Purring, she butts his leg with her head and then rubs her face against it.

Reaching down carefully, Leviathan scoops her up and drapes her across his massive shoulders. Despite her size, she easily and languidly stretches out across his shoulders and rests her head on her paws. Once she's settled, he reaches out and switches on his computer, typing in the number to reach out to the Blood Moon pack.

Ringing echoes through his office until an image appears, revealing eight burly bikers, each with varying degrees of anger on their faces. "Men, you have a mission."

Leviathan growls, his facial plates again shifting under his ebony skin. "An Omega has been abducted." Pausing again, his silver orbs flicker as his draconic slits expand and contract momentarily. He stares at the sheet.

"She's in her mid-twenties, about five feet, two inches tall. Pale-blue eyes and almost white-blonde hair like my mate, Celeste." Leviathan motions to the Snow Leopard on his shoulder. "The female in question is a Snow Leopard and an Omega." He punctuates every word, driving home the importance of the female's rank and status and placing this abducted female on the same level of importance as his own mate. To him, this mission strikes too close to home.

He waves the packet of papers at the camera and narrows his eyes. "My messenger will bring you the mission packet within the next thirty-six hours. Find her, bring her back, and save any others similarly held captive. You have authorization to kill on sight anyone involved in the abductions." Leviathan cuts the feed and kisses Celeste on the cheek.

It's all in the pack's hands now . . .

THE FEED CUTS from the TV in the clubhouse, and I'm left with more questions than answers. Looking over at the other men who make up the members of the Montana chapter of the Blood Moon Pack Motorcycle Club, I sense the mood is low. Unadulterated anger radiates from the guys, and distinct growls and grumbles echo through the room. It's frustrating to have to sit back and wait for assignments to be given to us. We know there are several shifter trafficking rings, and we want nothing more than to hunt them all down and end their reign of terror. We protect females in distress, and we won't tolerate anyone who abuses them. Many of us are also impatient to find our mates. But some of us aren't rushing to settle down quite as much.

Low growls coming from both Clutch and Claws warn that their beasts are on edge because of this mission.

There's nothing worse than a pissed-off brown Bear or Lion. "Let's wait to see what this packet says, then we'll do what needs to be done. We'll save the female and return her to her family." I lock eyes with each of my brothers to assure them we'll handle this. Sometimes, having a motorcycle club, or "MC," made up of mostly Alphas is not always the ideal situation. But thankfully, most of our Betas are generally laid-back and keep the Alphas from losing their shit.

The cracking of knuckles draws my attention to the other side of the room. "Good, so we wait for the Dragon to send the envelope and go." Clutch crosses his thick arms over his broad chest, rumbling deeply, and I can only imagine his Bear pacing in his head, ready to charge. His eyes flicker with the power of his huge Siberian Brown Bear. Whoever took this female is in deep shit if his mood is any indication.

I return my eyes to the now-blank screen where Leviathan appeared a few moments ago and begin to plan. "Get your road bags ready and bring anything you might need for this trip." Pausing, I glance down at my boots for a few moments, feeling my Wolf prowling at the back of my mind. "Prep the vehicles as well, in case it's worse than we initially thought," I add at the last minute. Better to prepare for every possible scenario and not need it, than to need it and not have it.

We need to find her, my Wolf says to me as he curls up in his place in my mind. His fur stands on end for several beats before lying flat against his body again.

Drawing in a deep breath, I head back to my office and sit behind my desk. I know he's right, but we can't do anything till we get that packet. Feeling powerless is not something my Wolf or I are accustomed to as the leaders of this rag-tag bunch. There are nine species of shifters in this club, each with jobs suited to their species' strengths.

You and I both know it's me who makes the others fall in line, my Wolf smugly declares from his corner of my mind. He sits up tall and proud and flicks his tail several times, thumping it on the floor.

Laughing to myself, I pull up the list of our completed missions. Hundreds of missions and females saved or rescued but still no mate for us. *Do you think we'll ever find her?* I ask my Wolf. He seems to be the only one with a game plan. I'm becoming tired of waiting for my mate. It's been so many years of searching.

My Wolf stands up and walks around before huffing out a breath. *Eventually, yes. At least I hope so.* I sense there's more under the surface than my Wolf wants to tell me. He's as tired as I am, waiting to find our mate. He returns to the corner of my mind and lies back down again, resigned to wait.

A knock on the doorframe snaps me out of my conversation with my Wolf. "What's up, little brother?" I glance up at my younger brother, Damon, as he stares at me while leaning on the doorframe.

A snarl escapes his lips as his eyes burn with the golden hue of his Wolf. Unconsciously, he raises his lip, and I see his descended canine. Shaking his head, he walks into my office and drops into the chair opposite my desk. "Just frustrated, man . . . So many females rescued and fresh packs we've visited. But neither of us have found our mates." Roughly, he runs his fingers through his hair. I watch my brother's agitation and see how this is wearing on him. He's coiled tighter than a top, ready to take off.

"Trust me, I get it. We're all getting older and none of us have mates. Yeah, the girls come and take the edge off, but it's not what our animals need." Shrugging, I lean back in my chair and stare at the ceiling, thinking of the meaningless encounters we've had over the years just to sate the human and the beast. Even my Wolf is feeling the pull of searching for a mate. "We need to be patient. Eventually, we'll find our mates. We just have to have faith." I try to say this in a way that will convince *me* as much as him. I want to believe my mate is out there, really I do. But I may need to accept the fact that it might not happen for me.

"How soon do you think we'll get this next assignment? I have a bike rebuild that needs to be finished by the end of the month. Just kind of need a clue, bro," Damon says as he looks between me and the phone in his hand. "I mean, I have time . . ." he says, shrugging and trying to take some of the pressure off me and the decisions I have to make.

Rising, I walk around my desk and over to the calendar on my wall. Studying it, I compare the dates for repairs we have scheduled with the expected arrival of the mission package. "If the messenger comes from the Hanged Man, he can get here within the hour. If he's coming from Leviathan's lair, it could be a day or two, three max." I turn back around to face my brother and see him nod his head.

"Hey, Boss!" Claws yells from the front of the clubhouse. "Charlie is on the horizon, walking a billy goat this way!" We hear the guys shuffling around the front of the clubhouse.

Quickly, Damon and I head to the front of the building. The sun is setting behind Charlie and the goat. Winter is right around the corner, and the temperature is dropping. The last of the leaves are falling from the trees, making the scene before us seem almost like a movie. But not just any kind of movie. It's like the opening scene of a horror movie, where the man on the horizon—or in this case, the goat—is walking to his doom.

I step out of the clubhouse, waiting for Charlie to arrive with the goat and the envelope containing the information we need for this mission. As it always does, my heart rate quickens in anticipation of the mission. But I know my guys inevitably get their hopes up, only to have them smashed when the female or females we rescue are not anyone's mates.

"Charlie! Good seeing you again, man. How's things?" I extend my hand out to him, and he seizes it, shaking it firmly. He's jumpy, as usual, but he's gotten better each time he arrives at our place.

"Pretty good, Trigger. Here's the information for your latest mission and a goat named Rorry," the flight shifter says as he looks around nervously as all the guys gather around.

I take the envelope and the rope tied around the neck of what looks to be a huge genetic misfire of a goat. Its ears are damaged, and it looks to be cross-eyed and keeps its head tilted to the side. But the strangest and most hilarious thing about it is the damn thing has its tongue hanging limply out of the side of its mouth. It's the dopiest looking billy goat I've ever seen in my life.

Claws takes the goat from me and leads it to the back of the clubhouse where he'll hand it off to our cook. Just as I turn to ask Charlie a question, he shifts on the spot and takes off, flying back to his home base.

I roll the envelope up in my hand and shove my way through the men and head back into the clubhouse. Striding down the hall to the meeting room, my stomach fills with dread. I know these females need us, and they need to be rescued, but how many more missions can we endure without any of us ever finding a mate? My top four men enter the office and close the door behind them, taking their seats.

Unceremoniously, I dump the contents of the envelope on the desk. A five-by-seven glossy of the most beautiful female I've ever seen floats down last and lands on the desk, facing me. Her pale-blue eyes and almost white hair capture my gaze and, apparently, my Wolf's attention as well. *Is she ours?* my Wolf whines, looking at the female staring at us.

I can only hope so. I pick up the picture carefully and spin it to face the others. "According to the demographic sheet, her name is Fiona, and she's a Snow Leopard who was adopted by the Targus pride." I continue to study the demographic sheet and recite the pertinent information to the guys.

"Prez, want me to call Titan? He's the leader of the Targus pride," Claws asks, his eyes glowing with the power of his Lion. He waves his cell phone in my direction, waiting for my response.

"Not yet. Let's do a little recon first before we get his and his mate's hopes up," I say quietly, not wanting to prematurely send my guys off on a rampage. Claws nods stiffly, looking from the picture in my hand and back to the phone in his.

"Understandable. Titan would descend on us faster than we could anticipate. There's no stopping him once he's involved," Claws states flatly as he looks between me and the paperwork on the desk.

"Exactly. Let's wait till we have solid leads before we bring him up to speed." Hopefully, my statement placates Claws long enough to gain a better insight into what we're facing.

ONE MINUTE, I'm minding my own business, picking winter wheat in my father's field. The next thing I know, I'm suddenly dizzy, then waking up here, locked in a cage. I'm seriously regretting my decision to go out alone right now. Daddy Titan always says females shouldn't travel anywhere unescorted, just in case. I'm starting to see the value in his warnings and his rules now that I've been abducted.

The bars of my cage are thick and closely spaced together. I can only assume they know I'm a feline shifter and can slip through nearly anything. Other cages surround mine and hold other females of different species. This cluster of cages seems to contain felines and perhaps a few Foxes. Across from me, there's a Wolf in a cage, pacing back and forth, and she looks super feral and furious. Talk about a real bitch. Next to her is a small

Desert Fox, curled into herself in a ball, and beside her is a Gray Fox.

Most of the females around me are in their animal form, but I don't know exactly why. I assume being trapped and held in cages has set their animals on edge and shifting was the best way for them to cope. Honestly, I can't blame them. Squatting here in my own cage, I feel vulnerable with no weapons in my human form.

There's a large chalkboard with all the species listed on it. Numbers are written in front of each species name, and then a second number is written after the name. I can only guess what those numbers mean. None of this can be good for anyone who's trapped here. By scent, I can detect the presence of male Oxen, Hippos, and what I think are a few reptiles. These males are larger and much stronger than I am, and they give off a dangerous vibe.

Any way you slice it, this situation sucks. I wish I wasn't so headstrong and had listened to my family. I wouldn't be stuck in this damn cage, surrounded by cold metal with people who more than likely want to hurt me. A soft whine escapes my lips, and the males glance in the general direction of my cage. Shit . . . From what I can see, most of the caged shifters are Omegas, like me. Fuck . . . I think these are the traffickers Dad warned me about.

We seem to be in some sort of warehouse with dozens of cages all holding female and male shifters. I'm amazed at the number of different species collected in this one place. The obvious explanation, with this many Omegas being held captive, is that they're either planning to auction us off or worse. Some of these traffickers have Omega sex dens just over the border in Canada. If that's the case, this is the worst possible fate for an Omega.

My cage is probably the nicest, but then again, I only just arrived. In the corner of my cage is a bucket I'm supposed to use as a bathroom and a tray hooked to the bars with food and water. I'm starting to understand why most of the Omegas have shifted to their animal form. This is worse than the images I've seen of the conditions at the local zoo.

"Who's this pretty thing?" A male voice knocks me out of my inner assessment of my current situation. Three tall, burly men stand outside my cage. They reek of Oxen and tobacco, and they haven't bathed in days. I scrunch my nose and press my back to the bars on the opposite side of the cage. "Oh, come on, sweetness. Give me a little honey," the bald man says as he presses his cheeks to the bars and makes kissing noises at me. His friends laugh at his actions and the disgusted expression on my face.

"I wouldn't give you honey if you were the last male alive. I'd rather die alone." Striking out, I swat at him, allowing my nails to become claws and slice the tip of his nose. Scrunching my nose, I scoot back and press myself against the bars at the back of the cage.

"You fucking bitch! I'll gladly watch when you're sold as a sex slave." Sneering, he bares his teeth at me, then smirks. "We'll see who has the last laugh when I make you scream." He grips his crotch suggestively, giving it a bounce.

Pointing at his crotch, I laugh. "What happened there? Did you decide to stuff your Underoos with jelly balls? Or is that rolled-up socks?" I ask curiously as I stare at the mass in his hand.

His companions laugh at him, and he hauls off and punches the smaller of the two men. "Shut up, fucker! You and your mini-me get no play. Everyone wants a piece of me," the man holding his crotch says. He smiles arrogantly while his friend curses at the bigger male under his breath.

"With or without barbeque sauce? I hear smoked Ox is divine." My eyes shift to that of my cat, and my canines descend as I stare at him. A soft purr rumbles in my throat as I think about eating smoked meat.

"Just wait, bitch . . . All it'll take is a dollar and a dream to rail you soon enough." The bald guy finally releases his crotch and walks away. His friends pat him on the back, congratulating him on his retort.

"You can get penis growth pills for a dollar? That's outstanding. I guess Planned Parenthood must have stepped up their game." Before he's able to spin and charge, I shift to my cat form and turn, spraying him with urine before curling up in a ball. He's spitting and cursing and yelling all kinds of unintelligible things at me.

I couldn't care less. I'm far from home, and who knows whether anyone has noticed I'm missing yet. Picking up my head for a moment, I stare out the windows at the top of the metal warehouse. I can see the peak of a mountain, covered in snow in the distance. I'm definitely nowhere near my home. I hope my parents are okay, and they've called for help. Coiling up tighter, there's not much else to do but sleep and hopefully forget where we are. *They'll find us. You know Titan loves you,* my cat says to me.

He's the best dad a girl can ask for, I quickly reply to my Leopard. *Momma is probably going out of her mind with worry,* I lament as I lick my paw, trying to distract myself.

You know, Rose is loving all the attention with us gone, my Leopard growls.

Yup, must be nice to reinvent yourself every second to fit the current trends. She should have been born a Chameleon instead of a Lioness, I shoot back to my Leopard, and she snorts a laugh.

She's just jealous her coat isn't as pretty as ours. And the Montana winters don't bother us, my Leopard says, before curling up again. A nap sounds like a wonderful idea. Anything is better than staring at the iron that traps us.

Later that day . . .

Loud banging noises startle me awake. Yelling, crying, and screaming fills the air and has my fur standing on end. The odor of burned fur and fear overpowers every other scent in the building. Several cages are being carried out using metal bars to hoist them. The trapped Omegas scream and cry, begging to be let loose and some try to claw at their captors.

Shit has just gotten very real. If the bald man is correct, they'll have an auction here in the next few days, and we'll be sold to the highest bidder. On the far side of the warehouse, rows of chairs are being set up in front of a makeshift stage. My chest constricts, thinking about the possibility of what may happen to us next. Fear has me in a stranglehold, and I struggle to draw my next breath. This situation has just gone from bad to worse.

Pushing up on my hind paws, I try to squeeze through the bars again. I press my face and keep turning my head, trying to fit. I hop from side to side, trying every set of bars, hoping that one set may give way just a little and allow me to escape. But apparently, they planned for me to try this. The damn bars are too close together for me to fit through.

The girl in the cage next to me radiates sadness. She knows we're doomed to be sold. Squatting back down in the corner of my cage, I return to watching and studying my captors. I may be an Omega, but I'm surrounded by Beta henchmen, so I stand a chance of escaping if I can just get past those doors. I glance between the front of the building, where the double doors are, and the back, where there's a single window about ten feet off the ground. With enough of a head start, I know I can leap that high and sail right out that window into the unknown. I have to wait and bide my time and hope one of these stupid Oxen gets brazen and lets me out to show me off.

SCATTERED across my desk are the papers provided to me by Leviathan. It's times like these I wish the big guy would allow us to call him and have discussions about the information he sends us. "This here's your mission, blah, blah, blah," then hang-up is getting really fucking old.

The recon his people have done tells me the warehouse is in the valley on the far side of the mountain range, close to our home. It also tells me there's only one road in and out of that valley that may make this trip a lot more difficult than it needs to be. I fire up my computer and pull up my maps program. Scouring through the program, I study the topography of the area. Just as I suspected, there's only one way in and one way out. This is not gonna be easy in any way, shape, or form. My eyes lock on my two flight shifters, and I give them a single nod as they leave the room promptly to go prepare for their part of the mission.

"Boss, are you sure you want to send Ajax and Chap to go do this?" Claws asks with his head tilted to the side, staring at me.

"We have no choice." My tone is nothing short of irritated as I stare at him, trying not to lose what's left of my temper. "We need an up close and personal assessment of the situation before we go charging in there." Something is different about this mission compared to the previous ones that we've had. My eyes roam over to stare at the photo of the missing Omega. Her pale-blue eyes haunt me. I almost feel as if she's staring at me, searching for me, begging me to save her.

"If you think that's what's best, then I'll get everybody set up and ready to go, just in case." Claws turns his massive back on me and strides out of my office with zero fucks given.

Turning my gaze back to the recon information Leviathan sent us, I compare it to the image I have up on the screen. There are minor discrepancies between the images and the paperwork they sent. I make several notes here and there about what the best approach for them would be and pull up the one hunting app I have on my phone to figure out which direction and speed the wind is blowing.

I make another note that Ajax and Chap need to come in from the southwest in order to be downwind from the warehouse. Several more notes are jotted down before they return with Claws, discussing what time they should leave.

"Okay, so the dusk thing is brilliant. Your feather colors would hide your approach well." I spin the computer monitor to face them. I drag my fingers over the screen and activate the wind app to show them how the wind moves through the valleys.

"Hmmm, that could be a problem with the wind. I think we should come in from this direction instead." Ajax's finger drags across the screen, showing what he was thinking. Raising an eyebrow and seeing his point, I agree with the path Ajax has indicated, and the guys bump fists and leave.

~Ajax~

After we've loaded up the truck, Chap and I go over the plan several more times, studying the map side-by-side. Almost an hour and a half later, we arrive at the five-mile marker, and Claws parks the truck under an old apple tree. We get out and climb to the top of the nearest hill, giving us a view of the valley on the far side. We can see the illumination of the floodlights from around the outside of the warehouse from where we're standing. This will be even more difficult than we initially expected.

We strip out of our clothes and take flight. Gliding on the thermals gives us the advantage of being able to get in and out silently. We circle high above the building at least a dozen times, studying it and watching men come and go.

Eventually, we decide to explore the road in and out of the compound. On our way back in, we land in a tree on the far side to watch the warehouse without wasting our energy. From here, we can hear females screaming and crying from inside and watch as the double doors open up and a flatbed truck pulls up. Several cages are loaded onto the back of the flatbed, then covered in tarps and driven away. Thankfully, no Snow Leopards were taken away.

In the back of my mind, I know we're running out of time. I take flight again and circle the warehouse once more, spotting a small tree by a window on the backside of the building. It's a small window, so hopefully nobody will notice me sitting there. I land in the tree and hop across several of the branches until I'm even with the windowsill. Thankfully for me, Eagles have fantastic eyesight, and I'm able to study all the cages inside the warehouse.

About six rows in toward the middle, I see the face of our target pressing up against the bars, trying to squeeze between them. No one can mistake the coat pattern of a Snow Leopard for any other enormous cat. I watch her for several minutes, making sure there are no other Snow Leopards in the building. Once I've made a positive ID, I take to the air and cry out once, summoning Chap to me as we fly back towards the truck. I move as fast as my wings can carry me. We're running out of time, and I don't want to be the reason she goes permanently missing.

I shift back to human about ten feet off the ground and land in a crouch before running to my clothes and quickly dressing. "Wow. Settle down, Ajax. Where's the fire?" Claws asks me as he hands Chap his clothing.

"They've started moving the Omegas, and I spotted the one we're looking for. I'm concerned she may not have much time left in that building, so we need to move." Understanding crosses the big guy's face, and he runs toward the truck with the rest of us.

I think we break every traffic law possible on the way back to our headquarters. When we burst in the front door, Bruiser is standing inside with Clutch and Trigger. "We found the girl. We gotta make a plan. We gotta get out of here. We gotta go get her," I rattle off quickly, trying to make them understand exactly how dire the situation is.

Trigger's eyes flare, and he turns to run back to the office. Hot on his heels, the rest of us follow him, not a single word spoken as we break into the room. Using the smart

TV, he throws the map up on the screen, and Chap and I show him where everything is on the map.

A quick search online turns up a blueprint for a similar model of the warehouse. Several clicks later, Trigger throws the blueprint up on the screen. I step forward and draw the locations of the specific cages, the doors, and the windows so everyone has a complete picture before them. I've never felt so rushed or worried in my life. Those girls are being held by one of the biggest Oxen smuggling rings we've ever found. Trigger fires off a text to Leviathan, giving him a mission update and, as usual, receives no response back.

"Ajax, I need you to go back with Chap and monitor the compound," Trigger says to me, and we turn to load up again and head back. At least this way, if we see something happening, we can call the club and get help within the hour to save these females.

As we're driving back toward the warehouse, I see the corner of Claw's eye twitching. The fact that a rare female feline who's also an Omega, like his little sister, has been taken has hit a personal nerve with him. The truck ride out was tough, sitting in silence with a large Lion shifter who's about to lose his mind in the driver's seat.

Arriving at the site again, I stop and glance at Claws and see his Lion's power glowing in his eyes. He turns his nose to the wind and breathes in deeply, closing his eyes. "You guys need to get going, just in case. I'll leave a charging block here for you to use if you need to call. We'll be here tomorrow night, fully prepared to execute the rescue," he growls as he stares at me, the fire of his aggression burning brightly. Chap and I nod solemnly before stripping and taking off to do our part in this plan. We have to keep the females in our line of sight. It's our job to keep them safe till the calvary arrives.

ONCE THE GUYS HAVE LEFT, I take stock of the reaction of the rest of the club to the news Ajax relayed to us. They grumble back and forth, most of them angry we're not leaving tonight to attack. "Listen. I get it! Everyone wants to go now, but we can't. We do this the smartest way possible. There are too many lives at stake for us to rush in without a plan," I growl, letting my Wolf's tone fill my voice. He's as on edge as everyone else.

"Okay, I agree. We have to take the time and focus on getting in there and getting the females out in one fucking piece," Clutch says as the brown fur of his Bear ripples over his forearms that are as thick as a tree trunk.

Shaking my head, I move over to the drawing board and make a list of the information Leviathan gave us. On the other side of the board, I list what Ajax and Chap found when they did their own reconnaissance on the area. Both reports are similar and hold most of the same details. The main difference between the two is that Ajax gave a count of the number of vehicles on the property, and he learned there's only one way in and out of the building.

Pulling up the map program on the screen, I show everyone the terrain. "We'll be sitting ducks once we break the tree line heading toward the warehouse."

"What if we cut the power?" Axel says, pointing to the power lines going in and out of the valley. I examine the image of the warehouse and the notes of where Ajax and Chap identified cameras were mounted on the exterior of the building. Glancing between the notes and the image, I can't agree with just cutting the power.

"Only problem with that is that they'll know something is going on," Bruiser says as he draws his hand down his face, frustrated that this is the best we've come up with. Thankfully, my brother said exactly what I was thinking. I prefer not to tell someone their idea wouldn't work like they hoped.

"What if one of the bar girls crashed one of our old junkers into the utility pole and take out the power that way?" Murphy offers, looking over his shoulder toward the main part of the clubhouse. He returns his gaze back to me, waiting to see if the Wolf disagrees with the Wolverine.

"We'd need to send Candy to do it. She's one of the more distracting girls we have on payroll here," Bruiser says as he runs his hand through his hair, looking back at the layout of the road coming into the valley. "She'd have to hit the pole on the main stretcher road at the end of their dirt road to make it look believable." He motions to the pole in question and then looks back over at Murphy. As the guys talk about the plan, I look at the map and think it sounds feasible. I nod, agreeing it's a decent idea.

"I'll go talk to her now and see if she's willing to crack up one of the old cars in the lot." As soon as he says this, Murphy turns and walks out of the room, not waiting for anyone to disagree with him.

"On to the next order of business, we'll need to divide ourselves up into two groups to launch a successful attack." I wipe the dry-erase board clean, making room to divide up the club. I split the guys up and make sure that everybody is aware of their part of the plan. The front entrance needs to be 100 percent covered. We're sending the prospects to the back to sneak through the little window that hopefully no one will be paying attention to.

We pull out the nondescript van we have as well as the extra truck we keep on site just in case one of the bikes breaks down. We load up duffel bags containing extra sets of clothing as well as blankets and extra terrycloth robes we recently bought. According to the head count

Ajax and Chap gave us, there could be thirty Omegas in cages in that building.

I stare at our van and decide it's probably not going to be big enough to fit all the Omegas in. We call in a favor from our bartender and ask him to bring his big old Econoline over. Between the two vans and the truck, we should have more than enough room for everyone. My only fear is that between tonight and tomorrow night, they'll move those Omegas. Let's face it, thirty Omegas, depending on species, can unfortunately be extremely lucrative in the right market.

My stomach turns, and I nearly vomit at that thought. Shifting gears, I refocus on planning how to get everyone out as safely as possible, going over the schematics of what the warehouse should look like, according to what Ajax told us. Since the building has only one way in and out, they must have reconfigured it at some point from the original design.

With Ajax's guesstimate of thirty, I figure there might be a maximum of forty Omegas and a minimum of twenty. Either way, that's a lot of bodies to move in a short time. I can only hope we don't receive any phone calls from Ajax, telling us they're on the move early and we have to leave before we're ready. It's now that I lay it out on the line. "The Bears and Wolves will charge through the front door, gaining the primary attention of the traffickers. All other shifters will come in after us and focus on freeing the Omegas from their cages so at least they can defend themselves. Claws, your priority is to go straight for Fiona and get her out." The Lion shifter gives me a single nod. I continue staring at the picture of Fiona and her haunting pale-blue eyes, and my Wolf begs me insistently to act now. He must instinctively sense something is going to happen and that we can't wait until tomorrow. He's never been wrong before, so I have to trust him now.

"Change of plans, boys. Pack up. We head out in five. We'll hit them hard and fast just before midnight. I don't want it on my conscience that any Omegas were sold because I hesitated." My guys cheer before running out of the room, preparing to leave immediately. I can only hope and pray with the number of Omegas in that building, some of my guys will find their mate tonight. If not, I'm not sure how much longer we can continue doing this and keep our hearts intact.

Clutch has stayed behind while the others left to get ready to go. I look to him, waiting to hear what he's got to say. "Why aren't we just busting in and taking out all the traffickers from the start? They all need to die. I don't get why that's not our plan."

"Settle, big guy. Not everyone has your size and strength. We also don't know exactly what shifters we're up against. We have to look at the long game, not the short one where everyone, including the Omegas, die." I try to be firm with Clutch. Lord knows I don't need a one-ton Siberian Brown Bear pissed off at me.

"Fine, we leave now. Kill the traffickers later. It's a good plan," Clutch says before walking away toward the vehicles. I guess the conversation is over, and it's go-time.

I DON'T KNOW what the fuck snapped in that dog's head, but for once, he got his head out of his ass and listened. Before I make my phone call, I walk over and double-check the vehicles and supplies. Everything I feel is essential for this mission is already loaded into the vehicles, ready to go.

This will be one of the toughest phone calls I've ever made. Titan is one of my oldest friends. Hell, he became leader of his current pride about the time I started getting my mane. He taught me what it meant to be the protector of a pride and how important it was to protect the females. At his behest, I joined the Blood Moon pack to help rescue females. This is the one MC who I know has their hearts in the right place and do everything in their power to do what's right.

I dial his number and listen to it ring. "Leo! Any word on Fiona?" His deep rumbling voice sets my Lion on edge.

Two Alpha male Lions cannot stay in the same territory or they risk fighting to the death. My beast waits anxiously to hear a threat or challenge from our old friend.

I take a few seconds to organize the thoughts in my head before speaking. "Ajax saw a lone Snow Leopard in a cage at the warehouse. We're going in hot tonight to bust the females out." My voice holds nothing but respect and yet a tinge of my Alpha rank seeps through. I scan the others, seeing the positive reaction from the guys.

"Do you want me to mobilize the pride as backup?" Titan asks, wanting to be involved in his adoptive daughter's rescue. I hear the hopeful tone in his voice, and it makes my heart swell to know he'll back us up.

"We've got this, my friend. Besides . . . I may get lucky and find my ole lady in one of those cages." I half-heartedly huff out a laugh. Part of me has given up looking for my mate and relegated myself to being alone for the rest of my life.

"It'll happen when it's meant to happen, Leo. Oh, I almost forgot. I gave the Omegas in the pride safe words." I can hear him rustling papers around before he laughs. "Fiona chose 'taffy' as hers." A chuckle escapes him as I hear more papers being shuffled around.

I arch a brow as I pull the phone away from my head to stare at it for a moment. "Are you fucking kidding me? Taffy?? Why the fuck does she need a safe word? Is she in a dynamic we're unaware of?" I'm wondering if Titan is hiding some twisted sex den on pride lands with the use of safe words. The hair on the back of my neck stands on end at the thought of it.

Titan snorts. "No, there's no dynamics here. I instituted safe words just in case we needed to send someone from outside the pride to pick a female up. If no safe word is given, they'll run. It's that simple. Fiona may be an Omega, but she'll claw the fuck out of you." He may be laughing, but I also hear the pride in his voice when he speaks about his adopted daughter.

A chuckle escapes me, thinking about this little hellcat trying to claw the fuck out of someone. Running my fingers through my thick hair, I tilt my head to the side, looking around. "I'll try to remember to use her safe word so I don't die by her claws." I picture her tiny Leopard attacking my Lion. The minor battle I'm imagining cracks me up, and I laugh out loud.

Now Titan laughs, apparently also thinking about little Fiona attacking my Lion. "I can't believe that she picked 'taffy.' Of all the things in the world, she had to pick that. And you! I can't for the life of me picture you saying 'taffy' to get her to follow you." Titan laughs harder, almost unable to breathe. The thought of me uttering that ridiculous word is funny, but I'll never let him know I agree about how comical it is.

"Laugh it up, furball. I'll send a catnip bomb to the pride when you least expect it." Wickedly, I grin, thinking about the bomb detonating and covering the compound in catnip. I brought an ex-marine buddy of mine in on the construction of the last bomb. It worked flawlessly, coating a majority of the compound in primo catnip.

An audible gasp escapes Titan's lips. "No . . . Not again! Last time you did that, three months later, we had a baby boom. Dozens of kittens at once and exhausted Lionesses everywhere . . . Not cool, man, not cool. I was praying for Bast to strike me dead in an act of mercy." The worry and concern in his voice is refreshing to hear from the usually unflappable Alpha.

Laughing, I end the call and head back to the others. The bomb was revenge for the catnip-lined refrigerator box he sent me for my birthday. I was so fucked in the head, I forgot how to shift. Fucking Clutch had to hose the box down to get me to come out of it.

"What's that look for, Claws?" Trigger asks. He's prowling around the room as if he's stalking all of us.

Rolling my eyes, I tilt my head to the side. "Remember the Great Catnip War of 2018?" I bite my bottom lip, trying to hold back my laughter and nod as Trigger's eyes widen. He stifles the laugh he wants to let loose.

"Oh . . . yeah. That box was hell. That bomb you made, though, was pure genius." Laughing, he leads me to his truck, and we hop in, heading toward our destination.

Using CB radios, we review the plan and the team divisions. I have the best and worst part of it all. I have to head straight for the female, avoiding the major fight, which is completely against my nature.

An argument ensues over the radio about why I'm going in first, even though we've been over it a million times already. "I'm sure a Snow Leopard will be thrilled when a random Wolf, Bear, or Hyena approaches her cage. Lions adopted her . . . Use the head on your fucking shoulders for once, assholes," I growl out, pushing my Alpha influence behind it. I'm over going around in circles and rehashing the plan, even though I'm the best option we have.

Trigger finally has enough of the argument and puts his foot down. "There are thirty plus females in that fucking warehouse, and you're fighting over one. What if your mate is a few cages over and you miss her?" he asks. His normally powerful tone is firm but has a hint of despair.

"As the only Lion in the club, I'll take the chance of missing my mate." I huff out a sigh, resigned to my fate of ending up mateless. I stare out the window, watching the scenery whipping by.

The rest of the run is silent as we approach the target. Parking five miles out, we make our approach downwind and on foot. Every step weighs heavily, thinking about the fact the others may find their forever.

Ajax crouches down, looking into the valley. Trigger whistles, getting him to turn and join us. "No changes since we last spoke. Looks like a skeleton crew of mostly

Oxen and two Hippos left," he reports, still looking over his shoulder, trying to monitor the building.

Size-wise, only Clutch and I are big enough to take on the Oxen. But the Hippos are a completely different issue. "Want me to get Titan here with some of the pride to take out the Hippos?" I say to no one in particular. Let's face it, the Lions are better equipped to handle the Hippos than the Bears and Wolves.

Trigger paces, thinking it over. "Make the call. Hippos will be a problem for us. It's better to be safe than sorry." I nod and walk away to make the call. Happy that Trigger has finally seen the value of the pride coming to help us.

Titan picks up on the first ring, laughing. In the background, I hear the whine of the turbo on that old diesel bus of his. His mate can be heard in the background. She's giving us both hell about her baby needing her and making threats about balls hanging off rearview mirrors and other male maiming I can barely make out. I turn back to the others, cradling my crotch, protecting my jewels.

"Titan was already en route with eleven Lionesses, his mate refused to sit by and wait for Fiona to be returned to them. There may be many castrations on the horizon." Collectively, the guys cringe, listening to me. Pacing back and forth, we wait for Titan to arrive. My Lion is itching to break loose and rip into anything that gets in his way.

A small bus pulls up with Titan and his mate walking out in human form. The other ten Lionesses have already shifted and are ready for battle. We need no words at this point, and those that were still in their human forms shift and start prowling toward our target. The mission is clear, and the target is in our sights. Time to go rescue the females and find Fiona.

SCREAMS AND BANGING around me wake me from sleep, and I sit up, looking around. New males, reeking of Alpha, are in the building. The traffickers begin pulling females out of their cages so these new males, who are presumably purchasers, can be afforded a closer inspection.

Kicking and screaming, the females shift to their animal forms in an attempt to keep the purchasers from touching their human flesh. My heart thundering in my chest, I watch in horror as some of the females who have shifted have collars slapped around their necks and are tied to a nearby pole.

The sharp, bitter scent of fear fills the air as females in nearby cages shift and start fighting, trying to escape their cages. My fight-or-flight instinct consumes me, and I know I need to get the fuck out of here. I desperately wish Titan could find me, but it's not looking like that's going to happen. I should have listened to him and taken a Beta with me when I went into the field. Regret nearly strangles me as I shift, pushing myself back against the bars on the far side of my cage that abuts another cage. I look behind me to see the female in the cage behind me shifting along with the others around us in a simultaneous wave.

The prospective buyers become angry at the shifting females, yelling and using their Alpha powers to try to force the females to shift back to our human forms. Some of the weaker females shift on command, but not all the Omegas shift back, which further pisses the men off. The power suddenly flickers and goes out, sending all of us into a panic. Screams and growls fill the air and heighten the fear level throughout the warehouse. Thankfully, as a cat, I see better in the dark than some of the others.

The irate buyers return the Omegas they were inspecting back to their cages while mass confusion ensues. The Oxen bark orders, and someone leaves to go investigate. The levels of stress, anger, and fear continue to rise dramatically in the warehouse, and I tremble, pressed as far back in my cage as I can get.

After what seems like an eternity and I'm nearly hyperventilating, I hear a Lion's roar in the distance. I know that roar . . . Titan has come for me. I bellow out, trying to answer him as best I can and let him know where I am. Other female felines respond to his call as well, causing alarm among the Oxen shifters.

The Wolves and other canine shifters begin to howl in unison, joining the felines in our calls for help the only way we know how. I have a strong feeling we're about to have to fight our way out of here, especially if Titan brought the pride with him.

When a second roar rings out, the fur on the back of my neck stands up. My mate . . . My Leopard perks up, no longer terrified. Curiosity overtakes my fear as I pace the cage, trying to get a glimpse of what's happening. It seems Titan teamed up with another dominant Lion. I wonder if there are two prides out there and if they're prepared to fight the Oxen and the Hippo shifters hired to watch over us. For the first time since I was abducted, my hopes rise. Looking around the interior of the warehouse, I notice an Eagle watching us through the only window.

Rearing up, I stick my paw through the bars of my cage, trying to get its attention. I keep waving my paw through the bar until the Eagle finally tilts its head, looking at me. He spreads his wings and presses his beak to the glass. Pulling my paw back down between the bars, I tilt my head so I can watch him closer. He turns his head, then looks back at me before taking off. Inhaling deeply, I sit back down on my haunches, waiting and watching the door. The Oxen and Hippos move quickly around the interior of the warehouse, checking lord knows what. I can only hope that Eagle was a shifter, and he's part of the rescue effort.

A smaller Lynx shifter is behind me, trembling against the bars. Her ears are pinned tight to her head, and she's curled into a tight ball, terrified. Hoping to provide her with what little comfort I can, I snake my long tail through the bars and wrap it over her. After a moment, she picks her head up and looks gratefully at me, then snuggles under my tail, hiding herself.

Several loud blasts reverberate through the warehouse just before the front door flies off its hinges. The biggest, scariest-looking Brown Bear in what is likely the history of Bears fills the doorway, looking like hell itself spat him out. When he turns his head toward the cages and his eyes meet mine, it hits me like a punch to the gut. He's mine too. That monstrous Brown Bear is one of my mates. I always assumed myself having only one mate. Having two isn't so bad and is something I can handle.

Apparently, being an Omega has its advantages. Multiple mates will mean multiple hunters and well-fed kittens. Contentment spreads through me with that thought. Pulled from my internal thoughts, I watch the expression of rage fill the massive Bear's eyes, and snarling, he goes to war, tearing a swath through the Oxen and Hippo shifters. In his wake, Lionesses from Titan's pride flood into the warehouse, viciously attacking the shifters guarding the Omegas. Lions were built for this shit, and they're destroying the stunned guards. They take team-work to an entirely new level, attacking the Oxen and Hippos in groups of two and three and taking them down with ease.

I'm so engrossed in the battle waging around me, and the Bear tossing an Ox around like a rag doll, that I don't immediately notice the Lion at the door to my cage. His deep, rumbling purr grabs my attention, however, and I instantly become lost in his golden eyes. This is the male whose roar called to me earlier. The scars covering his muzzle, as well as one frighteningly close to his right eye, tell the story of his violent life.

Slowly, I rise and walk closer to the door of the cage and run the soft pad of my paw down his nose. His scent envelopes me, and I'm strangely hungry for—of all things—freshly baked brownies. My mouth waters as I stare into his large golden eyes, seeing myself reflected in his gaze as he stares intently back at me. Just as my purr starts, he shifts into his human form. He's built like a mixed martial arts fighter, and whoa, his cock will more than satisfy a girl. Damn, I got lucky in the mate department. The Eagle I saw earlier swoops down and drops keys in front of my mate.

"My name is Leonidas, 'Leo' for short. Mom had a sense of humor," he says, chuckling as he tries keys in the lock of my cage. A man nearby yells for "Claws" to hurry, and my mate promptly flips him off. "Claws is my name in the club. Oh, I nearly forgot," he says as he finally gets the door open. "I was told to give you the word 'taffy,' so you'll know it's safe to come with me." His grin is teasing, and to be perfectly honest, I'd have followed him with or without the safe word.

The deep timber of his voice calls to something within me, and for the first time in my life, I feel as if I'm finally home. Hesitantly, I step out of the cage, refusing to shift to my human form because of the fighting going on around us. Leo shifts back to his Lion and starts to lead me out of the warehouse until he's side-swiped by a charging Ox with two Lionesses on his back.

I suddenly hear a deep male voice next to me, yelling, "Come here!" I'm grabbed by the scruff of my neck.

I whine and whip my body around and hook my claws into the man's flesh, drawing blood. He screams as he grips my paw, trying to pry my claws from his skin. As soon as his hand comes close enough to my mouth, I bite down hard. He screams and whips his arm out, sending me flying. I slam into the wall, and the world goes black around me.

CHAPTER SEVEN
CLAWS

FORCING MYSELF TO MY FEET, I stagger for several steps before I can stand properly. As I run past the man who threw Fiona, I extend my claws and rip open his stomach, gutting him. He drops to his knees, holding his stomach, and futilely tries to stuff his spilled intestines back into his body.

A Lioness bellows, and I change direction to find her standing guard over Fiona, staring down an Ox. I jump to the top of a cage and use it to launch myself at them. Sailing through the air, I extend my claws, prepared to latch onto the Ox. As soon as I land on his back, I sink my teeth in. The coppery tang of his blood fills my mouth as my claws dig deep into his thick hide. Growling deeply, I force my teeth to descend deeper into his flesh.

The Ox bucks and spins, trying to dislodge me. Unfortunately for him, I'm much larger and stronger than the

Lionesses. Titan finishes off an Ox he's fighting and moves to help me. The Ox I'm on is already bleeding out, making the floor slippery and difficult for his hooves to gain purchase. Now, he's become aware he has two Lions to contend with and starts to panic. Titan briefly glances back at Fiona and his mate, then refocuses on the Ox.

Out of nowhere, a Lioness sails over Titan, using his back to launch herself at the Ox. Just as she clears Titan's back, the Ox rears up, obviously not thinking that through, and gives her a clear shot at his throat. Growling loudly, she sinks her teeth in. Realizing the Lioness and I have the Ox under control, Titan moves to stand protectively over Fiona, guarding her. The Ox eventually succumbs to blood loss, and once his body hits the floor, we release him. We move toward Titan and my unconscious mate. Shifting to my human form, I kneel beside Fiona and scoop her up in my arms. Titan also shifts and looks intensely at me for a moment, then nods slightly as he herds the others away from us. Looking up, I see Clutch and Trigger staring at Fiona and me. "Is she okay?" The big Bruin asks in a far softer voice than I've ever heard from him before. Arching a brow, I study him.

"Yeah. But we need to get her back to the clubhouse." My eyes don't leave Fiona as I stand and carry her out the door. Trigger moves ahead of us and opens the door of the SUV, and I slide into the back, still cradling Fiona. Trigger slides behind the wheel, but Clutch climbs in next to me and places Fiona's tail in his lap. I would have expected that to piss me off, but for some reason, it doesn't.

"I don't know how to tell you this, Claws, but she's my mate too," Clutch says as he gently pets her tail, not making eye contact with me. Nodding, I watch my fingers glide through my mate's fur.

Glancing up for a second, I see Trigger watching me in the rearview. "I'm guessing she's yours as well?" I'm not sure how she'll react to having a Wolf as a mate, but that's on him. Trigger nods and says nothing else. I watch him glance several times in the rearview and watch us. Honestly, it's kind of unsettling, watching him watch us. Meanwhile, Clutch's Bear rumbles softly beside me as he runs his large hand over her flank and down her tail.

Trigger drives carefully back to the compound, and eventually, she begins to wake up. I watch her pale eyes blink open and look up at me. Her fluffy paw reaches up and rests on my cheek as we stare in each other's eyes. The intense feeling of holding my mate in my arms hits my heart like a freight train. Instinctively, I bend my head down and nuzzle her face.

We scent-mark each other, and our combined purrs fill the cab. Clutch presses himself against my shoulder and stares at Fiona in awe. She looks up and over at Clutch and then repositions herself so she can climb onto his lap. She's still purring and rubbing her face against his. "What's she doing?" Clutch asks softly as he gently runs his hands over the back of her animal.

"She's marking you with her scent. It's her way of saying you're hers," I say, tilting my head and watching her interact with him.

"Oh, this is a good thing. Bears don't do this kind of thing," Clutch says as he nuzzles Fiona, her scent steadily growing stronger within the truck cab.

"I think finding us may have sparked her heat," Trigger says from the front seat. His knuckles turn white on the steering wheel, and I hear the engine roar as he slams his foot down on the accelerator.

The truck's increase in speed throws us back in our seats, and Clutch and I grip Fiona tightly to keep her from falling from our laps. Her purrs and rubbing intensifies as we hold on to her for the rest of the ride back to the clubhouse. I swear the old SUV took off like a rocket and the miles melt away faster than they should.

Cori is standing on the porch watching the horizon, waiting for us to arrive back home. Shaking her head, she ducks back inside the clubhouse and returns by the time we park the vehicle. In her arms, she has towels and a robe. Trigger and Clutch slide out of the vehicle first, then race over to open the door for Fiona and me. Once the door opens, Fiona leaps out and jumps into the bushes. Cori laughs, looking between the three of us and the bush. "She had to relieve herself. Chill the fuck out, boys." Cori has always had a way of settling our beasts.

Fiona steps out of the bush and looks at everyone. Moving to the porch, Fiona meows at Cori, who nods and opens the front door for her to pass through. Arching a brow, Cori turns and follows Fiona into the building, leaving the rest of us standing outside, dumbfounded.

"What the actual fuck just happened?" I ask, waiting for someone to explain this to me. Clutch paces and occasionally stares at the front door. "Probably girl stuff . . . Females do weird things. Female Bears . . . They'll fuck you up before they'll accept you. Full-on battle mode. You lose, you're unworthy." His Russian accent stresses the severity of what Bruin males must go through to be deemed worthy.

"Hold up . . . So . . ." Trigger paces then stops dead, suddenly staring at Clutch. "Female Bears attack the males to see if they're worthy, and you have to fight back? How the fuck is that okay on any level?" Trigger's voice raises several octaves, revealing his distress at this information. We continue discussing the subject much longer than originally intended.

By the time Clutch has finished explaining the bizarre mating habits of Bears, the rest of the club arrives with the other rescued females and starts helping them into the large barn in the back of the compound. The club girls take to the abducted Omegas, tending to their every need. I notice Bruiser and Chap are each taking care of a female while Murph is staring at the house and pacing anxiously. I wonder if Fiona has another mate she's unaware of.

CHAPTER EIGHT
FIONA

CORI IS EXTREMELY nice and hysterical. She reminds me of Miss Piggy with how animated she is. After she's sure I'm cleaned up and dressed, we walk to the back of the clubhouse and come to a stop in front of a door that's locked with several padlocks. When the final lock is opened, she throws the door open, and inside is a beautiful nest. The room has an arching panel of glass, like one I saw in an arboretum at the botanical gardens close to my home. The bed is covered in beautiful soft blankets and what looks like a thousand pillows. The room is decorated in soft pastel colors and glitter-covered accent pillows. Tiny replicas of what must be my mates' animals line a shelf on the wall.

"I prepared this room in case the boys were fortunate enough to find someone to love," Cori says softly as she leans on the doorframe. She exudes an aura of confidence, yet the look on her face betrays her apprehension.

This room, I guess, is her way to help convince whatever Omega the guys find to want to stay.

"It's perfect." The words fall from my lips as I stare at every little detail. I swear this woman is the Swiss Army knife of prepared people. The room has no other animal's scent in it, and I know in my heart that will soon change. I have an overwhelming urge to burrow into the blankets and soft pillows and fill the room with my scent.

Just before I take a step into the room, I hear Titan call my name. Turning quickly, I run, following his scent, and plow right into him, knocking us both down, as I turn the corner. Laughing, we fall to the ground, and he cradles me like he did when I was a little girl.

"How's daddy's baby girl doing?" Titan asks as he kisses my forehead.

Laughing still, I roll off and sit on the floor, looking at him. "Much better, now that you're here, Dad." I smile broadly and look around. A bunch of the bikers and females have gathered in the room where we're still sitting on the floor. Feeling nervous, I scoot backward and hiss, noticing all the exits are blocked. Being held in that cage really messed with my head. At this moment, my mom pushes past the crowd of bikers and shoves Titan out of her way to grab me and hold me tightly to her chest.

Four of the bikers clear everyone else out of the room and then take up posts, leaning against the wall and giving my parents time and space with me. I bury my face in my mom's hair, breathing in her comforting scent. In the background, I can hear my dad talking to the remaining guys about my reaction and reassuring them I'm okay. I never did well with crowds, and after being in a cage, my fear of new people is far greater than it was before. My mother threads her fingers through my hair, soothing me and nearly lulling me to sleep in her arms. Slowly, the tension drains from my shoulders, and I'm able to look around and take in the scene before me. I recognize three of the men standing with Titan. The fourth man is a mystery to me. But when he finally turns to face me and my heart hammers in my chest, I know he's mine as well.

I pull away from my mother and slowly approach the men talking with Titan. At only five-foot-two, all of them except the fourth man tower over me. My nose is working overtime, trying to separate his scent from the others. To my left, the Lion smells delicious to me, like freshly baked brownies. Next to him, the Wolf smells like that first cup of coffee in the morning. The demon Bear smells like decadent chocolate and sin, wrapped up in one package. The fourth is an animal I've never scented before. His scent is thick and musky, like an expensive cologne. Each man freezes in place as I circle them, carefully looking them over.

One of the most beautiful aspects of the Omega and Alpha dynamic is that even though I don't possess power through force, I nonetheless possess a unique power: I own their hearts completely. An Omega can make or break an Alpha. We can love them or destroy them by breaking their hearts.

I choose to walk up to the Lion first and look up at him. He's easily a foot taller than me, plus some. I crook my finger at him, and he lowers his head down to my level. Gently, I run my fingers through his thick mane of hair, and his deep purr rumbles in his chest. Smiling, I lean forward and press my nose just under his ear and breathe in deeply, memorizing his unique scent. He remains perfectly still while I do this, letting me adjust to being in his presence. I back up two steps, and he raises his head, looking down at me. Smiling, I move my hair and tilt my head to the side in submission to him, granting access to my throat. Slowly, he lowers his head again and presses his lips to the pulse point under my ear, showing me he accepts me. "Thank you Fi," he reverently says close to my ear before standing back and smiling. You'd think I handed him the moon and stars.

Carefully, I move to the demon Bear and stare at this mountain of a man. Up close, he's even more enormous. Titan pulls me back and whispers to me about how his species of Bear chooses their mates. Nodding slowly, I continue to stare up at him until Titan is in position behind him. When I get Titan's signal, I back up and run as fast as I can and bury my shoulder at his hips, pushing my full weight against him. With Titan on all fours behind him, the Bear falls back and over him with a loud thud, shaking the room from his impact. I launch up and go for his throat, biting him over his jugular and growling as I apply pressure. His huge hands encompass my ribs, and he strokes my sides gently. My purr escapes, and I release his throat and lick the small puncture wounds I created. Sliding my nose along his neck, I sniff him under his ear, learning his scent. He reminds me of the dark chocolate I'd get at Easter as a cub, and I smile at the memory before I attempt to sit up. My knees don't reach the floor when I straddle his barrel-shaped ribcage. His smile disarms me as he chuckles, "Well played, my princess. I am at your command." The bass in his voice calls to my beast, prompting me to lean forward and kiss his lips softly.

"Okay. Enough of that, little one," Titan says, lifting me off my Bear. "You have two more mates to meet, then your mother and I need to get the pride home." Blushing, I nod and adjust my clothing before turning toward the male that's almost my height.

I circle him several times before stopping and looking him in the eyes. "I don't mean to be rude, but what is your animal?" Furrowing my brow, I tilt my head to the side, still studying him.

Chuckling, he runs his fingers through his short hair. "I'm a Wolverine . . . Not the superhero type. The bad-tempered, hole-digging, attack-out-of-nowhere kind." He winces, describing himself to me. I nod slowly as I look him over again.

"Would you shift for me? I didn't get to see your animal earlier." Smiling, I watch his eyes light up at the prospect of me meeting his animal.

He darts out of the room, and I raise a brow, looking back at my father and Leo. "I think he's trying to show you respect by stripping and shifting out of the room," Leo muses as if it's an odd occurrence.

Then, a small brown-and-white bear-like animal stalks into the room. His long claws are the first thing I notice after the pattern of his coat. His tail is adorable and fluffy. I sit down on the floor, letting his animal approach me at his own pace. With carefully placed steps, he climbs into my lap and his heavy musk scent floods my senses. I run my fingers through his thick, rough fur. "He's not nearly as scary as the stories say Wolverines are." He lifts his head and licks my cheek before climbing off my lap.

Once he's away from me, he immediately goes on the attack against the Wolf in the room. The way he flattens his body and bares his canines gives me an understanding about why Wolverines are feared. I get up from my spot on the floor and move to pick him up. "Okay, you proved your point. You may be little, but you're mighty," I say, smiling, and the Wolverine calms down almost immediately.

JEALOUS DOESN'T BEGIN to describe how I'm feeling at the moment. Watching Fiona carrying Murphy around like he's a teddy bear turns my stomach. The others are snuggling in close, waiting on her hand and foot. Shaking my head, I lean back against the wall, watching what's happening around me.

"What's on your mind, bro?" Bruiser leans against the wall next to me, watching the others with my mate.

"She hasn't even come close to me. Is it because I'm a Wolf?" I arch a brow, looking at my brother and sigh. I know cats and dogs have a long-standing feud.

"I don't think that's it. Let's face it, you're kinda stand-offish, Ty," Bruiser says as he motions toward Fiona, who's playing with Murphy's fur while sitting on Clutch's lap.

I look closely at the group before me and watch how Fiona interacts with the other guys. Turning on my heel, I head toward the kitchen and put together a platter of finger food and drinks. Grabbing a cart, I load all the food onto it, then wheel it into the living room.

Arriving with the goodies, I watch everyone's noses pick up on the scent of the food. Fiona gently sets Murphy on the floor, and he runs off to shift back to his human form. "What's this?" Fiona moves forward and circles the cart.

"I figured everyone could use a snack to hold us over till dinner." Shrugging, I offer Fiona a plate, then pass out plates to everyone else.

"Good call, man," Claws says as he cracks open a bottle of water and offers it to Fiona. She takes the water with a smile and moves to the couch, taking a seat.

Nudging me, Murphy slides up beside me and offers me a plate. "Make your plate and go sit with her. Let her get to know you, Prez." Sometimes Murphy is a brilliant motherfucker.

I give Murph a bro hug, then make my plate and head over to sit next to Fiona. Silently, I place my stuff down and offer her a napkin. She kisses my cheek after accepting the napkin and starts eating. I'll take that as a win at this point. I watch her pick at the different meats I placed on the plate, every bite she takes pleasing my beast that we provided for my mate.

"Not to piss in anyone's Cheerios, but we didn't see anyone who would rank as a leader of that group," Titan says as he walks into the room and leans against the wall opposite of the couch. The rest of the guys shuffle around, reacting to what Titan has said. Fiona freezes and her brows furrow. She stands up from the couch and heads directly to where Clutch and Claws are standing. I get it. Pound for pound, those two are the largest and strongest in the club.

Fiona nestles herself under Clutch's arm and visibly shakes, fear rolling off her in waves. "I smelled reptiles mixed in with the scent of the Hippos and Oxen," she tells us, her tone trembling before Claws takes her away from Clutch and holds her against him. I can hear his deep purr all the way over here. A softer, silkier purr soon joins him as Fiona snuggles in closer to him.

"We need to stake out the warehouse. I'm sure the leaders will return, looking for their goods, especially when they don't ship out on time," I say as I stride across the room to stand next to Titan. "We need to get the other females somewhere safe in case they bring the war to us." Crossing my arms over my chest, my gut is screaming at me to send Fiona away with Titan and the others. I'm trying to be the leader everyone needs me to be. But with Fiona standing in Claws's arms, looking at me, I feel like I'm missing something. For once, I fear failure. Prior to this, I didn't worry about whether we were successful in our missions. Now, I feel as if the world— my world—would end if I fail in this.

Pacing has always helped me break loose whatever mental blocks I sometimes get when I'm trying to work something out in my head. So that's what I do now, trying to come up with a solution that will work to keep the females safe.

"What if they track the girls here or to Titan's pride?" Cori asks from the corner of the room, breaking free of Axel's embrace. "What if they attack us? Strategically, we're fucked here in this valley . . ." My heart freezes in my chest as I think about the problems we'd have defending our current location.

"Prez?" My brother draws my attention away from my impending panic attack.

"What's on your mind, Bruiser?" I decide now is as good of a time as any to hear what my little brother has to say. After all, he's come up with some brilliant plans before. Hopefully, he has one now.

Walking around the room, he stops by the bay window and looks out across the property. "Let's take the females to the pack lands. I know we haven't been home in ages and our old man may be sore at us for not visiting. We know there are at least two dozen able-bodied males who can fight and defend the females." Bruiser's eyes flash to that of his Wolf when he looks into the other room. He nods at someone, and before I can ask him what's happening, a timid female rushes to him. He wraps an arm around her shoulders and draws her tightly against his body.

Fiona's eyes light up. She moves to the female nestled up against my brother, and they hug each other. "She was being held in the cage behind mine. I did my best to try to make her feel safe," Fiona says quickly before moving to stand before me. "The pack lands sound like a good idea." She looks over her shoulder, then back up at me. "If there are woods and mountains, most of the rescued females will be able to hide if necessary." She reaches out and grips my hand tightly, getting her point across. Her eyes flicker between human and the pale hue of her cat. All these years, I've held mild disdain toward felines. But it seems my mate is changing that opinion.

Forcing a smile, I look down at my little mate and nod slowly. "Gather everyone up. Let's be ready to roll out in the next hour. We'll divide the females up and take some to the pack lands and the others to the pride lands. Once we're sure they're safe, we'll let Leviathan do what needs to be done." Slowly, I bend forward and kiss Fiona on the forehead before pulling her to me and holding her tightly. Her soft purr makes my heart swell with this first major positive sign from her. Her scent of freshly baked bread fills my lungs and makes my cock pulse with anticipation.

Giggling, Fiona pulls away and looks around bashfully. "Cori told me my heat is days away, so we better go get settled somewhere." Furrowing her brows, she looks incredibly adorable.

Double blinking, I look at the other three guys. We all wear the same mask of concern when it comes to the first heat with our Omega. "That settles it. Let's get moving. We'll each take different routes to get where we're going." Titan agrees with the decision to divide and take evasive maneuvers. He gathers his Lionesses to start sorting the Omegas, taking all the felines, except our mate, with him.

Once he leaves the room, my brother gets on the phone and calls our dad, making plans for our arrival. Our go bags are ready for all situations. So any packing my brothers and I need to do for this trip is minimal. I watch Cori leave the room, taking the females with her. We follow them out to gather our bags and load the vehicles. Once everything is packed, we load everyone up and get on the road. At the fork in the road, the vehicles split up and head off to their respective destinations.

SITTING in the back seat of the truck is, without a doubt, the most boring place I could be. Staring out the window, I watch the world roll past me. Some of the places we pass, I would have wanted to stop at under ordinary circumstances, but these circumstances aren't ordinary and stopping is out of the question for us. The vehicles begin to slow, and I watch our caravan turn up a dirt road to nowhere. The incline of the road slides me back against the seat, so I relax and lean back, watching the trees go by. Seeing the snow covering the ground perks up my Leopard for the first time on this trip. *Can we play?* she asks softly.

"Leo?" I lean forward and grip the seat in front of me, looking at the road ahead, and wait for him to answer.

"Hmm?" he asks with a smile before pivoting his head to kiss my cheek.

"Can I play in the snow where we're going?" I scoot along the bench seat to sit behind him. Leaning forward, I rest my head on the ball of his shoulder.

Leo leans his head gently on mine and laughs softly. "I don't see why not. Then again, we'll be in the doghouse . . . Well, Wolf pack lands," he says, raising an eyebrow and looking at me in the mirror.

"Oh . . . Will they chase me? Like, not in the fun sense." I cringe and shake at the thought of escaping the snapping maws of the Wolves.

Leo reaches forward and hits redial, and I hear Trigger answer the call. "Hey, Prez. The Wolves won't chase our mate, will they?" The tone of Leo's voice has become more serious than it was when we were talking.

"Hell, no! I won't allow it!" Trigger growls, and I hear him barking orders to his brother in the truck with him.

"Good. She wants to play in the snow when we get there." Now Leo's tone isn't as harsh as it was before.

"We can all shift and let our animals loose for a bit," Trigger says before barking out more orders to his brother.

Squealing with excitement, I dive back into the backseat and snuggle into the comforter the guys provided me with. Rooting my face around in the blanket, I smile, scenting all my mates. The brilliant males must have each rubbed it on themselves.

"Take a nap, kitten. We'll be there soon," Leo says over his shoulder just as I sink below the comforter. A nap sounds like a fantastic idea.

I'm not sure how long I slept, but I slowly wake up to the lack of sound coming from the truck. Peeking out of my comforter cocoon, I see the driver's seat is empty. I hear the guys' voices outside my window as they debate which of them is coming to get me. Sitting up quickly, I look out the window, then pop the door open. It's a beautiful winter wonderland here. Flinging the door open, I leap out of the truck into the snow and start running around, enjoying the cold weather.

"Someone seems happy." A baritone voice jolts me out of my revelry. Without a second thought, I launch myself at Clutch and cling to him for dear life.

Clutch laughs as his massive hands encompass my ribcage, stroking down my back, trying to soothe me. The deep rumble of his Bear calms me down, and I purr contently in his arms. "Fi, this is Gus, the Alpha of the Timber Wolf pack. He's also Tyson and Damon's father."

Pulling my head back, I look at Clutch, confused. Leaning forward, I whisper in Clutch's ear, "Who are Tyson and Damon?" I look around and can only assume they're in the club. But which ones?

"Well shit, Fi. We did you a real disservice. Tyson is 'Trigger,' and 'Bruiser' is Damon. You already know Leo. And well, my name is Boris. I know, I know—typical Russian name." When Boris smirks, I notice he has dimples on both cheeks.

"You have dimples under this epic beard!" I announce and move the hair around on his face to get a good look at the hidden dimples. He quickly puts me down and tries to guard his face from my prying fingers. I may be shorter than he is by a lot, but I give it my best effort.

Tyson comes over, saving Boris from my assault, and carries me back over to his father. "Dad, this is Fiona. She's Leonidas, Boris, Murphy's and my Omega." Tyson names his road brothers by their given names with pride. His father looks each man over, then back down to me, and his smile softens.

"It's a pleasure to meet you, Miss Fiona. Don't let any of these males rule you. You're their Omega. A good Omega makes an Alpha a better Alpha and a better man. A bad Omega can destroy a pack in a heartbeat," Gus says with a brilliant smile on his face. He reminds me of what I'd think a grandfather would be like.

"I'll remember that, sir. Thank you," I say softly, slightly intimidated by my mate's father. "Can I play in the snow now?" I look from Boris back to Gus. All it takes is a slight nod of his head, and off I go. I dive back into the truck and strip as quickly as possible. My shift comes quickly, and I soon have a paw pressed to the glass, meowing to get out.

Murphy is the first to my door, and he opens it wide. Leaping out, I feel the eyes of every single pack member and the other Omegas on me. Snow Leopards are rare in their natural habitat. And here in the states, there's even less of us. I bound around, happy to be in the snow. Out of nowhere, a Lion's roar echoes, and I know it's Leo. I call back to him and start running in the roar's direction.

Spotting Leo, I take to the trees and stalk him from above. His massive Lion sits on a snow mound, looking over the edge of the hill. When I make it to the tree closest to him, I leap, paws extended, ready to grab hold of him. But the fucking bastard must have heard my claws when I leapt because he turns just in time to catch me, and we roll down the hill together. He uses his cat's massive body to cage mine in, protecting me. When we reach the bottom of the hill, I shift back, still straddling his Lion. "Silly male, shift back. This looks perverted." Lightly, I slap his Lion's chest as he shifts to his human form under me.

"No one told you to shift out in the middle of nowhere on top of me." Leo's tone is huskier than usual, and the gleam in his eyes speaks volumes.

"What if I like where I'm sitting?" I look over my shoulder and can see the veiny length of his cock pulsing in time with his heartbeat behind me.

Laughing, he sits up and cradles me against him and kisses me. My heart thunders in my chest as I feel my core pulse in anticipation. "Not here, beautiful. You deserve a nest with all the trimmings and the softest blankets, not ice-cold snow." From the sincerity in his voice and the look in his eyes, I know he means it.

"Let's go back." Leo curls around me and kisses my lips softly. "Shift for me, baby. Let's go see your new nest." He picks me up like I weigh nothing and sits me on my feet. The moment my toes hit the bitterly cold snow, my shift swallows up my human form. A quick meow escapes my lips, and I take off running back to the pack lands. I wonder what Tyson has in store for us.

FIONA AND LEO'S cats can be seen breaching the horizon side by side. Excitement thrums in my chest as I pace, waiting for them to get back. My mom helped set up a nest room for Fiona the moment I informed her I had a mate. Her shock at the others also being in the mate bond quickly wore off when mom saw the guys with Fiona.

Fiona shows no signs of stopping as she runs as fast as she can in my direction. At the last minute, she leaps up and is airborne. Her paws are outstretched, and I swear there's a smile on her face. All hundred-something pounds of Leopard hits me full force, knocking me back onto the snow. Her purrs fill the air, and her rough tongue rakes over my beard and bare cheeks.

Gently, my finger threads into her thick spotted fur. "It's good to see you smile, son." My father's tone interrupts the magic of our moment, and Fiona bolts and hides behind Leo. Her cat, peeking from between his legs, looks out at us.

Sitting up, I close my eyes briefly at the loss of my progress with Fiona. I finally had her undivided attention, and dad scared her. Damn it to hell. Arching a brow at my father, I shake my head, slightly defeated. "Fiona, I want to show you the nest room my mom helped make for you." Standing slowly, I dust myself off and turn to walk toward what used to be my house. My parents did nothing with the house that was my home before I left, figuring when my father was ready to retire, I'd come back.

I open the door wide for Fiona to enter before me and motion for the others to follow. Once everyone is inside, I close the door, leaving lingering family and nosey pack members outside. Fiona's cat looks up at me and a soft meow escapes her lips. Taking the hint, I lead her to the bathroom on the first floor and offer her a terry cloth robe I keep in the linen closet. She follows me into the bathroom and then proceeds to headbutt me till I leave the room.

Closing the door behind me, I strike up a conversation with the guys, telling them about the house and what's where. I give them a brief history of the house, motioning down the hall in different directions, waiting for Fiona to emerge. Lithe fingers slide over my cheeks and up over my eyes. The weight of her body rests against my back as she struggles to cover my eyes. When I crouch down, she can finally do it with ease, and a giggle escapes her lips. Her velvet lips press to my cheek before she releases me. I watch her movements out of the corner of my eye. She comes to stand beside me and offers me her hand.

Drawing in a deep breath, I rise to my full height and scoop her up to carry her bridal-style down the hallway and up the winding stairs. In the small tower on the second floor, a memory foam bed sits in the circular space and is covered with pillows and the softest blankets I could find. "Is this for me?" Her voice hitches at the end of her question as she looks up with those pale eyes of hers. My heart shudders in my chest as I gain my composure enough to nod and motion her forward. A high-pitched squeal escapes her lips, and she dives headfirst out of my arms into the comforters and pillows.

The guys do me a solid and leave the room. Inch by inch, I get closer to the nest and kneel by its only exposed side. Fiona pops her head out and kisses me firmly on the lips. Her scent wraps around me, and it's sweeter than before, which shoots a bolt of lust straight through me. My beautiful mate has gone into heat. A soft whine escapes her lips as she paws at me, trying to pull me into the nest with her.

Climbing into her nest is no easy feat for me, and no sooner am I in, she rips my clothes off with her claws.

"Please Ty, I need you!" Her whine sets the hairs on the back of my neck on end. An Alpha's drive to please and provide for their Omega is all-consuming.

"Whatever you need, baby girl, I'll give you." My rumble comes from deep in my chest as I nibble Fiona's neck. She climbs on top of me, her slick heat gliding over my aching cock. I can already feel my knot pulsing, knowing it will soon be locked deep in my Omega.

Fiona has a wicked gleam in her eye as she leans forward and nips my bottom lip. Without warning, she slides back, impaling herself on my cock. Simultaneously, we gasp from the shock of it. Never in my life have I felt anything so perfect. Her core wraps around me like she was made just for me.

Several deep breaths later, Fiona starts fucking me like there's no tomorrow. Quickly, I grip her hips and meet her thrust for thrust. Her whine spurs me on, and I take control and flip her onto her back. I grip her hips again, holding her at the perfect angle to hit all her right spots. Her keening cries are music to my ears.

Panting and pawing at me, she keeps trying to be the one to fuck me, forgetting I'm in control. As soon as her orgasm ends, I drive forward and sink my knot deep inside her. Her muscles crush down on me, throwing me over the edge with her into ecstasy. Practically roaring, I keep thrusting, dragging out probably the most intense orgasms of our lives. Just when I think I can't take anymore, I lean forward, as she tilts her head to the side, and bite her shoulder, marking her.

The warmth of the first rays of sunlight after a storm has nothing on the mate bond. My entire body thrums with a warmth I've never felt before. The intense love my mate has for her Alpha humbles me. If I wasn't already on my knees before her, I'd drop down this instant and worship her.

Carefully, I withdraw my canines and tend to my mate mark. Fiona nuzzles my shoulder and starts licking it, wanting to bite me in return. Dropping my shoulder down, I gently place my hand at the back of her head, encouraging her to bite me. Her needle-like cat teeth sink into my flesh, stinging for a brief moment before the warmth spreads over me again. Our bond is fully sealed and settled. So much peace and affection surround me, I can honestly say I feel like I'm home.

My knot finally releases, and I slide free. "Let's get you cleaned up and fed." I kiss Fiona's forehead before sliding out of her arms and into the nest. The room I chose was part of the master bedroom that has a huge walk-in bathroom. The open floor plan of the second floor is perfect for our family. I start the water in the shower and place several shampoos and conditioners on the sink. I even have scented soaps and different kinds of washcloths.

I hear the soft padding of her bare feet across the wood floor and smile. "Is this for me, Ty?" Fiona asks softly, looking around the bathroom. You'd think she's in the middle of a fairy tale.

"This and more, baby girl. Enjoy your shower." I kiss her cheek and give her a light smack on her ass before leaving the room.

FUCKING TRIGGER COMES PRANCING downstairs painted with Fiona's scent all over him and reeking of sex. Murphy, Clutch, and I stare at him like he's a hydra. I know that scent. Our mate is going into heat.

"I guess you're having a good morning . . ." I growl, barely containing my cat's temper.

Clutch and Murph slowly back away from the table. The cat versus dog thing is very real. The fact he went in there and marked Fiona first makes my blood boil. "She literally took me hostage," Trigger says, raising his hands in a placating manner.

Losing my temper, I roar at Trigger before storming outside to go on a hunt. Fucking Wolves don't court right. You're supposed to bring your female a fresh kill to show you're worthy. Roaming the woods on the pack lands will also serve to relax me some.

After an hour, I come across a herd of deer. Stalking along the rocky cliff face, I single out a young doe who was more than likely born this year. My kill is swift and painless for the deer. Carefully, I cut open the stomach and shift back to my human form to clean and gut it for the trip back.

When the carcass is ready, I shift back to my Lion form and pick it up in my jaws. I practically prance back to the house with my prize. Thankfully for me, the door has a lever I can use with my paw to open it. Much to Trigger's dismay, I walk through the house, carrying my prize to our mate upstairs. Blood drips from the carcass and trails behind me as I head up to Fiona's room. I headbutt the door and enter her den. The room reeks of sex and the sweet perfume of my precious mate. The minute she scents my kill, she steps out of the bathroom toward me.

Fiona steps into the room, naked as the day she was born with all her goddess given curves on display. Bast blessed Fi with the perfect body for me. She has curves all over, as well as a beautiful swell to her belly that will be perfect to bear children when she's ready. Dropping the deer before her, I bow my Lion's head to her and back up, then lie down, purring and watching her inspect my kill. "You brought me food. You're so thoughtful, Leo!" She moves toward me, kisses my Lion on the nose, and scratches both of my cheeks.

Quickly, she shifts before me. Her Leopard is more beautiful to me each time she shifts. Sinking her canines into the meat, she tears at the flesh, and the ripping of skin is music to my ears. Her Leopard feasts on the deer, purring up a storm as she fills her stomach. I get up slowly and walk into the bathroom, shift back to my human form, and run the shower to clean up from my hunt. Just as I step under the water, I hear a sharp intake of breath from behind me. Looking over my shoulder, I see Fiona looking at me like I'm a side of beef.

Languid steps carry her across the tile floor till she reaches the glass that separates me from her. "Mind if I join you? I'm dirty." Fiona practically purrs as her eyes glow with the power of her Leopard.

"Of course, anything your heart desires, my love." The husky tone of my voice makes the hairs on the back of my neck stand on end. So this is what the beginning of an Omega's heat does to an Alpha. The thought of my Omega stepping into my shower with me makes my cock hard as steel. Bashfully, she presses the glass door open and steps in with me. "Do you want the water hotter or colder, sweetheart?" I hear the words fall from my lips, but they don't sound like me.

"A little hotter, Leo. Please." Fiona visibly shivers before me, and I pull her against my body, her small curvy frame fitting mine perfectly. She snakes her arms around my waistline and rests her head between my pecs. Reaching back, I turn the heat up and allow the water to hit me first till I feel it warm up. Fiona's purr ignites my desire, and I rock my hips gently, nudging my cock against her stomach. Her breath hitches, feeling me against her, and she tilts her head up to look at me.

The raw heat in Fiona's gaze undoes me. Quickly, I lift her up and cage her against the tile wall, using my body to support her. I bend down and capture her lips, pouring all the love an Alpha has for his mate into the kiss. Frantically, she kisses me back and the blooming scent of her arousal fills the shower stall, driving me nearly mad. Gently, I nudge myself against her sex and feel her gush at my first tentative thrust. I fight against my instinct to rut her into tomorrow. Our first time shouldn't be mindless and rough.

To my surprise, she pushes herself down, impaling herself on my length, and gasps at the thickness she finds. Her keening cry makes me bury my face against her neck and nibble the spot I plan to bite later. The first flutters of her muscles spur me into motion. Long, slow, drawn-out strokes slide my cock slowly in and out of her depths, every inch of me brushing against her sensitive nerves, making her moan and quake in my arms.

Her claws extend and hook into my shoulders, taking me prisoner. "Leo! I need you . . . Please . . ." I feel her muscles milking my length. My love is on the precipice and whining at me, and I fully intend to keep her there a little while longer. But then, the little minx leans forward and bites me on my right pec, and I thrust up hard into her, picking up the pace. Her orgasm hits her like a freight train, and she crushes my cock, practically strangling it. Heaven. I now know what heaven feels like. My thrusts come faster and harder as I bottom out, rutting her. Fiona's screams fill my ears, and I give in to my instinct and bite her bare shoulder, holding her in my teeth. Fire burns in my veins as I thrust faster, chasing my orgasm. Finally, I hit my peak, and stars erupt behind my eyes, every throb of my cock shooting streams of my thick cum deep within my mate, hopefully hitting its mark.

I flip our positions quickly, my back hitting the tile as I cradle my mate, stilling my motions. Our combined purrs are perfect to me, her soft sounds a compliment to my rough ones. Carefully, I release her shoulder and lick the wound I caused, marking her as mine forever. I feel her little needle-like teeth also withdraw from my chest as she purrs, cleaning me.

Reaching over, I shut off the water and wobble a bit, trying to stand. I feel like Jell-O—perfect, happy, content Jell-O. I'm so thankful for the layout of this room since the nest isn't terribly far from the bathroom. I make my way, carrying Fiona from the bathroom and over to the nest and lay her down in the middle of the soft blankets and pillows. When I'm sure she's settled, I head back to the bathroom for a washcloth and towel.

When I return to her, Fiona looks at me quizzically. "What are you doing?" She tilts her head, her eyes darting from the towels, then up to my eyes.

Shaking my head, I kneel next to her and begin drying her skin. "It's called aftercare, love. I guess I'll have to educate the Wolf later." Fiona smiles and lies back, stretching out before me and allowing me to dry her, then clean up her most intimate spots.

"I can clean that, Leo." She tries to snatch the washcloth from me as I make my first gentle pass over her sex.

Lightly, I bat her hand away and smile. "It's my honor and privilege to be your mate. It's also my duty to take care of all your needs." Understanding dawns on her, and she relaxes, allowing me to take care of her fully. My heart soars, knowing my forever is before me. I am really a lucky bastard.

NIGHT AND DAY. That's the difference between how Ty and Leo took care of me. Ty was quick to curl up and take a nap with me, holding me close in his arms. Whereas Leo showed me something called aftercare. He cleaned every inch of me and even gave me a massage after all that. I've never been made to feel so special in my life as I have in the last few days.

I wander downstairs, following Leo to the kitchen. The rest of the guys are there. Thankfully, at the moment, I'm not a sex-crazed maniac and can get something to eat. The guys freeze and stare at me as I enter the room. The only one who breaks out of whatever spell they're under is Boris. The huge Bruin is already at the stove, cooking something I suspect is for me. For such a large male, he's very graceful in the kitchen.

Murphy moves over to me and gently takes my hand, guiding me to the head of the table. "What would our princess like for lunch?" My eyebrows shoot up at the mention of lunch, and I look at Ty and Leo, puzzled.

Looking sheepish, Leo shrugs his shoulders and laughs softly. "You slept till noon, love. Don't worry, Clutch will make you something delicious to eat." He motions to Boris, who winks at me over his shoulder when I smile at him. I wonder what he's like? Is he rough and demanding or gentle and caring? I study the striations of his muscles as he moves around in front of the stove, cooking.

My train of thought is broken when Murphy lightly kisses my cheek. I blink at him and can't help but smile. "What would you like to drink, princess?" He directs my attention to the cart he's wheeled beside me. There are at least six pitchers of drinks arranged by color on the cart.

"What's this? It looks like orange juice." I stare at one of the pitchers and notice bubbles in the juice.

"That's a mimosa. My mom used to like to drink them with her lunch. I wasn't sure what you'd like." He goes through the rest of the drinks on the cart and waits patiently for my decision. I can tell by the way he acts, he's not an Alpha like the others, possibly a Beta in the pack.

"A mimosa sounds divine. It's five o'clock somewhere, right?" I laugh as the guys chuckle, shrugging as I raise my glass to my lips and sip at the refreshing drink. I moan in appreciation as the cool liquid slides across my tongue and down my throat. The bubbles tickle the roof of my mouth and bring a smile to my face.

Boris approaches and lowers a covered tray before me. "I hope you like it, little one." The husky rasp in his voice makes me wet, thinking about him and, well, all kinds of naughty thoughts. With a practiced flourish, he lifts the lid, and I'm assaulted with some of the most delicious smells I think ever existed. He's prepared a seasoned rare steak with bacon and eggs and hash browns as well as what looks like a gourmet rendition of mac and cheese. He's artistically plated everything, making it look delicious and visually appealing.

Without a second thought, I launch out of my chair and into Boris's arms, hugging him tightly around his thick neck. I must have shocked the big guy because we fall back. With an "Oof," he cradles me and protects me when we land on the floor. "Little one, are you okay? Are you hurt?" His hands slide all over my body, checking for injuries. The frantic worry in his eyes breaks my heart.

Tears fill my eyes as I look at this mountain of a man under me, afraid of my being hurt when he's the one who took the brunt of the impact. "I'm okay. I promise, I'm okay. You protected me." Sniffling, I lean forward and pepper his cheeks and face with kisses, trying to kiss away his worry and fear. I begin to purr as I nuzzle his cheeks, reassuring him I'm safe and uninjured. My hands ghost over his skin, trying to soothe away the worry creasing his brows.

Carefully he sits up, cradling me like a small child, and he hugs me tightly, yet gently. The power this man possesses, contrasted with how gentle he is with me, makes me feel even more special. Boris picks me up and carries me back to the table, sitting himself down in my chair and positioning me on his lap. Once I'm settled, he feeds me the lunch he cooked for me.

How on earth am I so lucky to have such a gentle giant for a mate? I kiss his cheek between bites, then reach out with a spare fork and feed him some of the food. It's significant when predators share food, and his eyes light up, becoming misty. I quickly kiss his eyes, hiding the fact he teared up over my gesture. I honestly want to embrace the fact that this terrifying Siberian Brown Bear is a huge softy underneath.

Boris smiles up at me and hugs me again. My purr deepens as I rub my face against his, marking him as mine with my scent. His laughter bellows as he holds me tightly to him. After we finish eating, he stands up and carries me through the house to his room. Gently, he places me on his bed, climbing up next to me and starts massaging my calves.

"Come here, my teddy bear." I extend my arms out to him, motioning my hands in a "gimme" gesture. He grins and slowly crawls up my body, kissing every inch on the way. He remains in plank over me, nose to nose, and I see the power of his Bear flicker in his eyes.

Reaching up slowly, I caress his cheeks and thread my fingers through his thick beard. His Bear rumbles contentedly, and a smile creeps across his lips as he stares down at me. "You are the most precious being in my life. The sun rises and sets because you deem it so." His sincere words and tone shake me to my core. My Alpha has essentially given me the world on a silver platter.

Curling up to meet his lips, I kiss him, trying to convey all my love and affection to him. He smiles mid-kiss and rolls us so I'm straddling him. "You have all the power, little one. Do whatever you wish to me." Boris's rasp gets deeper, and I feel myself gush with excitement. He moves his hands and arms up and places his hands behind his head, demonstrating how serious he is about me taking the lead.

"If you really mean it . . ." He nods his consent, ramping my excitement several notches. Flattening my palms, I run my hands under his shirt and up his stomach to his chest. Unlike Leo and Ty, he doesn't have washboard abs. Instead, his firm stomach has a softness over the muscle and a happy trail disappearing into his pants. As I move up his body, I brush my fingers through the light dusting of hair on his stomach that leads up to his thickly furred chest. On anyone else, I'd likely be repulsed, but on my mate—my Alpha—it's hot. Shifting a single digit to a claw, I grin, looking up at Boris. "I hope you're not attached to these clothes." His eyebrows shoot up right before I get to work stripping my Alpha.

CHAPTER FOURTEEN
CLUTCH

FIONA HAS that wicked look in her eyes which concerns me a little. Her claw rips through the fabric of my shirt like it's butter. Is it wrong that I'm hard as a rock and already pulsing and aching to fill my sweet Omega? Her tentative movements heighten my curiosity. Her light touches and the deep rhythmic purring let me know she's okay. She's just taking her time, learning my body and figuring out what she's comfortable with.

Fiona finishes cutting off my shirt and begins kissing and nipping my flesh. It's difficult to keep my hands behind my head and not put them on her. I can't help but rock my hips up each time she slides her little body over my denim-covered crotch. Giggles escape from her as she places her hands on my stomach. "Naughty Bear . . ." She playfully slaps my stomach and scoots back down to work on my belt buckle.

Planting her feet on the bed, she grips the leather tightly and is finally able to get my belt undone. Her lithe fingers work the button at my waist free, then she inches the zipper down. My breath hitches the moment the back of her knuckles brush along my hard length. I rock up against her hand, and she smiles, eying the top of my boxers.

Tilting her head to the side, she bites her plump bottom lip and nearly undoes me. I thought I was aching before, but now it's far worse. Her hands slide under the denim and work the fabric down my hips. "Lift, please . . ." escapes her lips between purrs, and I instantly comply. Oddly enough, she only pulls down my jeans and not my boxers. I arch my brow, looking down at her.

She gives me a subtle wink, then presses her face against the cloth of my boxers and nuzzles my length. I damn near choke, feeling her lips and face against my cock. My Bear watches our mate with rapt attention as she nuzzles every inch of us. I have an overwhelming desire to reach down and touch our mate, but I don't want to scare her. Fiona's claws come out again, and she shreds my boxers right off me. Her scent is thick, and her purr is broken, almost aggressive. "Boris . . ." She slides up and straddles me. Her panties are soaked, and her whine has me wanting to destroy whatever is hurting her. "I need you. I ache . . ." She tears at her clothes, trying to get everything off.

As soon as she made clear what she wants and needs, I spring into action and help her remove the offending clothing. I roll us till she's under me, and I lick and nip her skin, starting with her collarbone. Her moans are music to my ears. She threads her fingers in my hair, guiding me where she really wants me. My greedy little Leopard pushes me down her body, right to her core.

I glance up to my writhing mate and flatten my tongue before licking her slick heat all the way to that little bundle of nerves. She damn near flies off the bed with the first lick and thrashes wildly as soon as I suck her clit into my mouth. Quick flicks of my tongue over the sensitive tip has her moaning almost constantly. Carefully, I slip one thick finger into her and slowly curl it, hitting all the right places. Her internal muscles suddenly clamp down on my finger, taking it hostage as I assault her clit with my tongue. Her screams and pulls on my hair spur me on to lick as fast as I can. Watching Fiona come apart is the most incredible sight I've ever seen. The instant she shatters, my tongue is coated in her honey and makes this Bear want to root around for more.

I wipe my face on the sheet and climb up the bed, nestling myself between her legs. Gently, I inch forward, slowly sliding myself into her warm depths. We both gasp, feeling the completeness as the warmth of our bond wraps around our hearts. Rocking slowly, I inch myself deeper into my love. We moan and writhe together, grinding against each other and chasing the feeling. Her walls flutter around my shaft, begging me to pick up the pace. Fiona's whine kicks up again, and I go mad from the urge to rut my mate.

"Boris, please." she whines and claws at my back. I can't deny my mate. I withdraw from her and flip her over quickly. She automatically raises on all fours, presenting herself to me. My heart thunders in my chest, seeing her full round ass in the air and the glistening of her lips, begging to be filled. I knock her knees closer together, making her tighter and harder to get into. Several swipes of my length have her whining again. Without warning, I sink balls-deep into her and set a punishing pace. The sound of wet skin slapping fills the air as the headboard slams repeatedly into the wall, leaving indentations, no doubt.

A high-pitched scream escapes Fiona's lips when her orgasm hits her like a freight train. Her internal muscles crush down, nearly strangling my cock, flexing and pulsing around me and making it hard for me to hold off anymore. My Bear roars as I bury myself deep within my mate, and my cum pumps into her with each of my thrusts. Reaching forward, I hoist her up and sink my teeth into her shoulder. Interestingly, I notice a tiny teddy bear tattoo peeking out from under her hairline.

After one last thrust, I sink myself balls deep, feeling our combined throbs prolonging our orgasms. Wrapping my arms around Fiona, I hug her tightly, feeling the love flow freely between us through our bond. Our animals are content, and I'll be fucking honest, this is the calmest my Bear has ever been. The Bruin is curled up in the corner of my mind, content as fuck. Gently, I lay us down and reach carefully for the covers and draw them over us.

When I soften and slide free of Fiona, she turns in my arms, nuzzling my chest and curling up. Her purr softens and settles out as she wraps an arm around me. I'm the luckiest Bruin alive. I have my perfect mate as well as my friends in the bond. Life simply can't get better than this. Pressing a kiss to the top of her head, I close my eyes and sigh contently.

Something in the back of my mind, however, compels me to remain vigilant even though it appears we won. It was far too easy. These traffickers have been in business for several years, but in all our prior rescues, we've never seen reptiles in charge. Something doesn't sit well with me. Maybe it's because my Bear is possessive. Maybe it's because we've busted those assholes so many times before and yet, they keep coming back. It's becoming sickeningly tiresome. After this nap, I'll pull the guys together and figure out what the actual fuck is going on.

As much as I want to rest and enjoy this moment, I cannot completely relax. I can't get my mind off the traffickers. The next conversation with the guys will not be happy or joyful. Part of me wants to go on the offensive, to hunt these fuckers down. But that would leave our mate unguarded, and that's an unacceptable option. These questions flood my mind as I ponder exactly how safe we really are. Gods, why do I have to be so paranoid?

I FEEL it the moment Clutch becomes part of the bond, and before that, when Claws did. It's a strange feeling each time. I know an Alpha feels all the pack-mates within the pack. It's how a pack works. The Alpha feels everyone. I'm not sure which of us is the most dominant Alpha, but I know everyone in this bond has each other's back.

Dinnertime rolls around, and Murphy and I prepare the meal. We're not 100 percent sure what Fiona will want to eat, so there are several different choices of meat and vegetables along with a side salad. Claws arrives shortly after I finish plating the meat and setting out the serving plates.

"Hey, Trigger. Can I lend a hand?" Claws sits on the island, waiting to help.

Looking around the kitchen, I motion to the cabinets at the end of the counter. "If you can grab plates from the last cabinet and set the table, that would be great." I smile briefly before returning to take the food from the oven.

"No problem." Without hesitation, he grabs the place settings and gets to his task.

I stand where I am for several beats, watching Claws work before returning to my task. Murphy moves beside me to prepare the salad. The moment Fiona wakes up, my sense of her in the bond flairs to life. It's brilliant and feels like a warmth wrapping around me. Claws pauses his movements about the same time I do, and we look at each other and pick the process up.

I set the last of the food on the table seconds before Clutch and Fiona make it downstairs. "Wow, guys! This looks delicious," Fiona says, rushing to look at the food we've set out. After she finishes her lap around the table, she hugs and kisses Claws and then me.

During all this, Murphy stands to the side, appearing to study his shoes. Fiona turns in his direction and barrels into him, nearly tackling him. Laughing, they hold onto each other while trying to keep their balance. Murphy grabs hold of the island countertop to stop them from falling. Fiona continues playfully laughing as she tries to climb him like a tree. Shaking my head, I wrangle her away from Murphy and hand her off to Claws. "Let's eat and try to regain some semblance of strength and sanity," I chuckle as we head over to the table.

"Actually, we have a problem . . ." Clutch says, crossing his arms over his chest. It's rare the big guy speaks out, so the rest of us freeze in our tracks and stare at him.

"We never found the ringleaders of that group. And to be honest, I noticed some of the females we got out this time, we've rescued before." Clutch's blunt tone makes me stop and think about this latest group of females.

"Fuck, you're right. Several of them are the same." Running my hands through my hair, I look over at Fiona and stare at her. "Murph, we need to get in touch with that biologist you know. See if they have some type of scanner for tracking devices." My blood runs cold, thinking about whether we may have inadvertently led the traffickers right to my father's pack.

Quickly, I text my brother and Titan and warn them about our suspicions. Soon, I hear my brother's truck firing up behind the house. His shouts echo throughout the compound as he mobilizes the females we've brought here. In approximately an hour, he has them in the truck and en route to the Hanged Man. I send a text to Leviathan, letting him know all the rescued females are headed to his bar and he needs to search them for tracking implants. All I receive back from him is an emoji of a flame.

Boss man can't say we didn't warn him about the trouble inbound to his bar. Hopefully, we're wrong and just paranoid. I'd rather be overprepared than not prepared at all. The colder climate here is not a favorable environment for reptiles. But then again, evolution is what it is. Hell, look at Claws. African Lions shouldn't be comfortable in the cold, and yet, here he is.

Two hours later . . .

"Son . . . Intruders have been spotted about five miles out. Looks like they brought Oxen with them this time. Wolves aren't equipped for this," my father says, having joined us to let us know about this new development. He shakes his head and looks out the back window. "We have an hour, at the most, before they arrive." He turns back to look at me, and I see the concern in his eyes.

"Get the females and children to safety. We just need to slow them down to allow the rest of the club to get here. Titan said, after they drop the Omegas off, he and the Lionesses will be here in force." Pacing the kitchen, I walk around the island, then look out the window, standing next to my father.

Dad rests his hand on my shoulder and gives it a slight squeeze. "I'm proud of the man you've become. I may not agree with the biker decision, but you guys are making a difference in the world." Most of the time, my brother is the golden boy in Dad's eyes, but hearing he's proud of me makes me feel invincible.

"Clutch, I need you to guard Fiona. Don't leave her side, no matter what happens." I move to the Bruin's side and place my hand on his shoulder. He gives me a firm nod and looks out the window behind him.

"We'll shift and move into the forest. At least there, we'll have our senses and claws to protect ourselves." Clutch kisses the top of Fiona's head and ushers her out of the room for a moment.

As I'm about to delegate tasks to the others gathered in my kitchen, I'm tackled by Fiona's Leopard. All one hundred and twenty pounds of her feline takes me to the floor like I weigh nothing. Laughing, I try to keep her enormous paws from smacking my nose repeatedly. Eventually, she climbs off me and licks the side of my face, purring as she leaps up onto the island to watch the others.

"This is my mate, Fiona." I motion to her, then look back at the Wolves gathered around the kitchen. "There are Oxen shifters inbound, and I'm fucking positive they're a distraction from the actual attack." Glancing at my father and my bond mates briefly, I turn back to the pack. "Keep your head on a swivel and watch each other's backs. Titan is bringing his pride here to help out with the Oxen problem."

"We don't need fucking cats here!" one Wolf shouts out. Fiona stands up and roars, then she hisses. Her head whips around to Claws, and the rage on his face concerns me.

"Here we go. Dog versus cat again. Fucking moron. Have you ever fought an Ox shifter? No? Sit the fuck down and shut up." Claws's voice roars with his dominance, and over half the Wolves sit immediately. A second later, the other half wobble, then sit.

Fiona leaps off the counter and nuzzles Claws's hand, encouraging him to pet her. Shaking my head, I look back at my birth pack. "Like it or not, it's not your choice who my mate is. I won't tolerate speciesist pieces of shit in this pack." Usually, I'll let bullshit fly, but this is one topic I won't allow to fester within the pack.

"Be prepared. The Oxen are coming, and we'll have a fucking battle on our hands till Titan gets here." The Wolves flood out of the house, half of them shifting on their way out the door. We outnumber the Oxen we know about. What we don't know is if they're bringing backup.

CHAPTER SIXTEEN

MURPH

IT'S SUPPOSED to be my time with Fiona, our moment to start our forever. Instead, we're preparing for war and a faceless enemy. I follow Boris and Fiona into the forest, far away from where ground zero should be. My animal is nowhere near as large or formidable as the others, and it pisses me off.

I'm almost embarrassed to be her mate. What the fuck do I have to offer her? My shifter form is small and surly, and I'm not anywhere close to being as strong as the others. Shaking my head, I follow Fiona and Clutch up the side of the mountain, still in my human form. As the terrain becomes steeper, I'm finally forced to shift. Fiona's cat turns and stalks back to me, circling. She's never seen a Wolverine, and it's painfully obvious how much smaller I am than her.

Reaching up on my hind paws, I show Fiona my claws. Gently, she bumps her nose against my paw, then examines me even closer. I feel like I'm under a microscope the way she's looking me over. My stomach tightens as bile threatens to surge to the surface. What if she deems me unworthy? What if she rejects me because my animal is smaller than hers? What if I can't protect her? Then she kills me herself? Her cat's rough tongue comes out and licks the side of my face, shocking me back into reality. A reality that my mate is larger and, pound for pound, deadlier than I am.

Shaking my head, I land on my paws, then nudge her to follow Clutch up the mountainside. What else am I supposed to do? The Bruin is much better at protecting her than I am. He has the size and the strength to crush a car if he wanted to. The roar from Claws's Lion stops us dead in our tracks, and I look back down toward the houses. All-out war wages as Oxen thunder through the town, nearly trampling the Wolves in their path.

Fiona turns to run downhill, but before she can take a step in that direction, Clutch gently picks her cat up by the scruff of its neck and carries her up hill. Shaking my head, I follow the Bruin up the hill to a pile of rocks. Behind the rocks, there's a small cave out of the line of sight of the houses. Clutch sits Fiona down and motions for her to go into the cavern. I tilt my head several times, then move forward and enter the cavern first. The opening itself appears to be just barely big enough for Fiona to shimmy herself into, which will be perfect to hide from large predators.

Fiona still protests entering the cavern. Clutch must have shifted to his human form because I hear him explaining to her why she needs to get inside. Eventually, she relents and climbs into the cavern with me and looks at the opening as if, by some magic, that one-ton Bruin would fit in here. The space inside is cramped, and for once, I'm thankful to be as small as I am. Fiona's cat paces around the interior, growling under her breath. In the back of the cavern, I smell something warm and moist, and I can only hope it's something worthwhile. Working my way around the rock formations, I make my way to the back of the cavern. Lo and behold, there's a small hot spring in an opening about the size of a regular bathroom.

Rushing back to the front of the cavern, I bite the end of Fiona's tail and try to drag her back with me. She whips around and tilts her head at me curiously. Motioning with my head, I turn and head back to my discovery. Thankfully, I hear Fiona following me over the loose rocks and into the area where the hot spring is.

"Well, fuck me. There's a hot spring in here!" Fiona says as she walks naked to the water's edge.

Shaking my head, I shift. "Well hell, if all it took was a hot spring to get you naked with me, I'd have bought a hot tub." I laugh softly at the look she gives me—half irritated, the other half full of mirth.

"Oh? You think you're tough, Murphy?" She raises an eyebrow, looking at me.

I was raised to think Omegas were docile, sweet little ladies who preferred their Alphas big, strong and dominant. But here I am, a short fucking Beta with a mouthy five-foot-two hellcat for my beloved mate. "I reckon I do. I may not be an Alpha, may not be able to mark or knot you like an Alpha. Hell, my shift is a surly little bastard." I enter her personal space and rest my hand against her neck and look into her eyes. "But everything I've got is yours. My heart, my soul . . . My damn life, if you want it. I'd lie down this minute and die for you."

I watch as her pupils dilate, then shrink to pinpoints, and then dilate again. "You don't need to die for me, Murphy. Live for me." She raises up onto her tiptoes and kisses my lips softly. "Dying is easy, Murph. Life is so much harder to endure. Live for me."

Her words strike a cord deep inside me. I'm about to shed a tear over the words my mate just spoke. My heart is damn close to beating its way out of my chest, thundering like a thousand hooves pounding over the plains of my family's ranch. I would die for this woman right here, yet she wants me to live.

My life has held no meaning up until this moment, a moment when my shift and my lack of stature don't matter. Before I realize what I'm doing, my lips crash down on hers, and we cling to each other as if we're starving. We back into the waters of the hot spring and continue pawing at each other. Fiona climbs up my body and then arches her back and slides my cock deep inside her.

She stiffens for a moment, then looks at me. Surprise is written all over her face. What I lack in height, I make up for with the size of my cock. Grinning, I lean forward and kiss her lips. "Surprised?" I ask as I tilt my head to the side, watching various expressions flicker over her face.

"Fuck, you should warn a girl you're packing a python. Or is your daddy a horse and I wasn't made aware of that?" There's that sass I've come to know and love from Fiona. Tentatively, she moves on my length, trying to adjust to the size of my cock.

Pride swells in my chest at her reaction, and I blush slightly. "No, my dad definitely isn't a horse. I'm just lucky, I guess." I grip her hips and begin thrusting slowly up into her.

Nuzzling my cheeks, she smiles and nips my bottom lip. "I'm the lucky one," she says before burying her face in the crook of my neck as she tries to muffle her cries from her orgasm. Her muscles pulse along my length, milking every inch, causing my balls to draw up. A tight coiling has started in my lower stomach, and I know I won't last much longer. Water sloshes all around us as I drive up harder into Fiona, chasing my own completion.

Growling, I lean forward and bite her shoulder with my human teeth, holding her in place on instinct alone. Every pulse of my cock buried with in her spurs her orgasm to renew its intensity. Several soft thrusts later, I'm spent and never felt better in my life. My mate is in my arms and our bond thrums softly in the background. After a moment, I carry an already sleeping Fiona up to the shore and lay us down on the sand. Her head rests in the crook of my shoulder, and I drape her arm over my chest. If there wasn't a war waging outside, I'd say today was perfect.

CHAPTER SEVENTEEN

CLAWS

OX AFTER OX charges in from every conceivable direction with no signs of stopping anytime soon. The thundering of hooves is nearly deafening on the frozen earth. We're severely outnumbered, and unless something changes, we're in deep shit. I can only hope and pray Titan shows up with the Lionesses and the young males of his pride sooner rather than later. The Wolves are taking a beating, and to be honest, I've almost eaten a horn or two when I wasn't looking. Just when you think you've learned their pattern, they change it up again. It's not as if they're charging consistently. They're coming at us with a hit-and-run offensive, which is extremely difficult to defend against.

This isn't the first time I've faced Oxen, and it probably won't be my last. They're herd animals, after all, and want revenge when you kill one of their friends. Today alone, I've dispatched four of them to meet their maker earlier than planned. If only we could figure out which one is the leader and take that one out, it would throw the entire herd off, not having someone to bark orders at them.

Roaring my frustration, I charge back into the fray. Claws swipe out indiscriminately as I attack every cloven-hoofed animal I pass. Blood coats my fur, turning it crimson and matting it down in places. My face and mane are painted red like war paint as I bathe in the blood of my enemies. This battle feels like it's been waging for days instead of hours. The Oxen have the size, and it almost feels like they may have the numbers to completely turn the tide and run us into the ground. I can't let the others realize just how dire our situation has become, fearing it may cause more harm than good.

Off in the distance, the sound of twin turbos echo through the valley, and the whine of a diesel engine spooling up gives me hope. Titan has apparently busted out his hauler and is transporting his entire pride here to help play cleanup. Over the ridge, I see the smoke from the stacks of his rig, and my resolve strengthens. We will win today, without question. The air horn of the truck sounds, quickly followed by the roars of the Lions he brought with him. Roaring back, I answer their calls and bolster the drive of the Wolves and my club brothers.

The wide-eyed fear on the faces of the Oxen makes my sadistic feline heart jump with joy as they try to escape. The Lionesses and the young males surround the pack houses, trapping the Oxen within the borders. On Titan's signal, the blood bath begins, and they leave not one single Ox standing. Body parts and entrails litter the roads and sidewalks, and strangely, some hang from low tree branches.

Walking with purpose, I grab my discarded clothing and dress enough to be presentable when meeting up with Titan. "Excellent timing, old friend." We shake hands and look out over the carnage his pack caused in the town square. A few stragglers still run through the streets and are being pursued by Wolves and Lions.

"Just like the old days with your father. Blood and guts everywhere and not an enemy left standing," Titan's voice booms, and his words make me miss my father. His broad smile and the way he's puffed out his chest remind me of my father after a battle. Strong and proud and without an ounce of ego when it came to his abilities in a fight.

Nodding, I think about his words and remember the stories my father used to tell. I look back at him. "Dad's stories about the savanna and where our people came from put all this into perspective." I motion to the bodies littering the ground before us. Heavy horned male Oxen are truly a difficult foe to defeat.

Titan places a hand on my shoulder and beams with pride. "You held this town with a bunch of Wolves, who aren't equipped to fight Oxen. That's impressive, son. Be proud of yourself." The ever stoic and regal Titan softens for a moment before returning quickly to his serious self.

"I appreciate your help, as always." I step in for a quick bro hug, then back up as if it didn't happen. Both of us glance around, hoping no one witnessed our soft moment.

"You did the pride a solid. Several of the young males found their mates within the group of Omegas you had me take with us. I guess it's time to look outside our borders for mates for our children." He nods slowly, motioning to the females now emerging from his rig. "We removed trackers from several females. The others appear to be clear. Where's Fiona? My mate brought the scanner with us to check her over as well." Titan scans the buildings and the surrounding tree line, looking for Fiona.

Closing my eyes briefly, I focus on the bond between us. A smile graces my lips before I look back over at Titan. "Apparently the Wolves have a hot spring they were unaware of in the mountain." I chuckle to myself over that minor fact, then realize there's a new tether in the bond. "Hmm, seems like Murph was a mate as well."

Titan laughs, then looks toward the mountain. "Your Beta is one of her mates? Fiona will tear him apart." Titan turns to walk away. "When Fiona returns, have her see her mother. She'll take her to get the tracker removed." With a wave over his shoulder, Titan returns to his pride.

There's still no sign of any leader on the horizon, only minions running around doing their master's bidding. A literal herd of foot soldiers slaughtered, their flesh torn from their bodies by the claws of my people. A couple of dozen misguided Oxen lay dead, painting the dirt vermilion and the air with the stench of their musk.

Walking through the streets of the pack's land, this place reminds me of the way my father set up our pride. Families live in clusters within the pride and are able to take care of everything. Even after getting their manes, the males knew the queen was who ruled the pride. Hell, the females run everything when to comes to the pride and its functions.

Something in the air changes. It's a scent that shouldn't be here. Spinning around quickly, I scan the horizon, trying to catch where the scent was coming from. "Crocs! Spread out!" I bellow, running through the town. How could I have been so blind to the fact the Crocs were behind this? The cold weather alone should have been enough to deter them from being here.

I look over at Trigger's Wolf. "We need to get up the mountain. The Crocs are here for Fiona." My shift is instant as my paws hit the dirt with a renewed sense of purpose. My mate is in danger and up in the mountains, far from my reach. Snow is the bane of my existence and makes travel more treacherous for a desert-dweller like me.

The bellow of Clutch's Bruin echoes down to us from the mountainside. Hearing the bellow, Titan's Lion roar sounds from behind me, and I can only guess he's hot on my heels. Closing in on the sounds of battle, there are at least a dozen Crocs scaling up the mountain.

Blood and retribution fall in line behind the drive to save my mate. The fact I can't see Fiona scares me. I can only hope the guys have hidden her well to keep her out of harm's way.

WHAT THE ACTUAL fuck are these dinosaurs doing climbing the mountain? They're fucking purses, armed with razor-sharp teeth. They meet every slap of my claws with the snapping of giant jaws and countless numbers of teeth narrowly missing my fur.

Dozens of these long, scaled, toothy creatures climb up the side of the frozen mountain, heading toward where I've hidden my mate. Every time I think I have one defeated, two more take its place. It feels like there's no end in sight. I'm one Bear against at least a dozen of these creatures I've never faced before. In the distance, I hear the roar of the Lions, and I know that Claws is on his way. Hopefully, he's bringing back up 'cause these stupid motherfuckers don't wanna die. My claws barely penetrate the heavy armor of these creatures. Thankfully for me, I'm more agile than I look for my size. I've barely escape getting chomped twice in the last few moments. I can only hope there's no way these creatures can get into the cavern where Fiona and Murphy are hiding.

With that thought, I back up the mountain and over toward where I've hidden them. I know their animals could slip into the hole in the mountainside. I just hope these scaly assholes are too big to fit.

I finally get a good swipe on one of them and break its bottom jaw before it's able to clamp down on my opposite paw. Blood turns the snow pink in spots and red clots litter the area just under the dinosaur.

Reaching down, I grab the injured creature and start using its body as a weapon. I've locked my jaws around its neck, and I'm flinging my head side to side, beating its comrades with its armor. The cavalry arrives, and thankfully, the Lions know what to do with these creatures. I think they may be Crocodiles, but it seems they wouldn't be this far north, given how cold it is here. Unless, like the Lions who live here, they've adapted to the colder climate. Either that or it's because they're shifters that the cold doesn't affect them like it would their natural counterpart.

From deep within the cavern, I hear the yowl from Fiona's Leopard. I want to get to her, but there's no way my fat ass is fitting in that tiny hole. Even if I shifted to my human form, my shoulders are too broad to squeeze in there. Unfortunately, I believe the worst has happened and some of these Crocodiles found their way into the cavern. I can only hope Fiona and Murphy can outsmart these reptiles. Otherwise, I'm afraid of what may happen since none of us can get to them.

~Fiona~

I'm as big of a fan as the next girl of watching all the nature programs on TV. In particular, the ones where they show the cute little fluffy babies running around tackling each other. This is not one of those programs, and I am not the girl to manage being attacked by a freaking Crocodile in the middle of Montana.

Thankfully for Murphy and me, Crocodiles can't climb very well, and there's enough of a rocky outcropping in here for us to gain some serious height and get to safety. But what we didn't expect is that several of them would be on foot as humans above us and would drop weapons down to their guys who are shifting back to human.

"Here Kitty, Kitty, Kitty, Kitty," one Crocodile shifter says, bent down and acting as if I'm a house cat. I seriously think this dude bumped his head when he fell down out of the ceiling and landed in the water. There is no way I am ever going to come to the "Here Kitty, Kitty" thing.

Of all the dumb things these traffickers could have done, resorting to some of the old human pet feline relationship skills? I mean seriously, dude, I'm over one hundred pounds. My species is endangered, and I totally don't trust you. I hiss at these guys and swipe my paw in the air, showing off my claws at them.

Four of the men laugh. "Better watch out, boys. We've got ourselves a spicy one here. She thinks she's all big and bad with those little pretty kitty claws." The man's southern drawl almost makes what he's saying adorable. Unfortunately for him, I'm not into cold-blooded reptiles who steal Omegas and sell them on the market.

Refusing to shift back, I slowly climb higher, making my way around the interior of the cavern. Unfortunately for me though, I can hear the men have backup just above us. So if I make it to the top and I'm able to jump and grab onto the opening, I'll be grabbed by the scruff of my neck, ripped out of the hole, and shipped off to who knows where.

The safest thing for me to do at this moment is hang tight, lie low, wait, and hope for the cavalry to figure out that there's a second way into the cavern. Then get my fuzzy ass out of here. Murphy and I keep looking up toward the opening, hoping the men leave.

A Lion's roar sounds and echoes in the cavern, and I know that roar is Titan's. I get antsy, listening to the scuffling going on outside of the hole above me. Murphy and I inch closer to the opening, trying to see what's going on just out of our eyesight.

The next thing I know, a body goes flying over the top of the opening, ripped to shreds, and dripping viscous fluid down on us. I take this moment to launch myself at the opening, to get myself out of this hole and into the fray. Several more bodies go whipping over the hole and are followed by a giant Lion. Using my claws, I pull myself up and out into the snow above. Several Crocodiles still surround the Lions, each one snapping its jaws dangerously close to the members of Titan's pride.

Seeing my opening, I take a chance and launch over the top of one Lioness and land on the back of the Crocodile. My claws barely gain purchase on its thick, armored hide. My last ditch effort is to sink my teeth in, just behind the lizard's skull. Unexpectedly, the Crocodile goes into a death roll and nearly dislodges me from its back.

Without a second thought, I release my grip on the Crocodile and jump out of the way, only to watch Leo fly past me and tackle the Croc I injured. They roll and tussle in the snow, painting it with the Crocodile's blood. I hear the sound of ripping and then a pop as Leo severs the Crocodile's head from its body. The minute he drops the Crocodile's head, I run to him, excited and relieved we're finally being rescued.

If it's possible, I swear his Lion broke out into the biggest and brightest smile I've ever seen. His deep purr brings me comfort and warms my heart, making me feel safe at last. Then, remembering I left Murphy down in the cavern, I turn around quickly to look back down the hole

I just climbed through for him. His little brown fluffy face and sharp teeth smile up at me. I don't know how good of a climber a Wolverine is, but I'm pretty certain he's going to need a lot of help to climb up here with the rest of us.

IT'S TIMES LIKE THIS, I'm grateful I broke with tradition and bartered peace with Titan's pride. The Wolves and the Lions have an accord that anytime either the pack or pride need assistance or support, the other provides it without question. So far, my current dealings with Titan's pride had been quite beneficial for the pack and my club.

While the other Wolves and I finish cleaning up down here, the Lions make their way up the mountainside to follow Titan and Leo. My gut tells me that up there, a secondary force is attacking where my mate is being held for her protection. But what my gut is also telling me is that whoever is the leader of this fiasco wouldn't hit us head-on like that. That individual is probably going to be a sneaky motherfucker. That fucker is probably planning to sneak into town and lie low while the forces go after his minions up on the hill.

With a minimal motion of my hand, I send Ajax and Chap to the skies to keep an eye on the pack and the pack lands. If anybody is gonna try to sneak in under the radar, it would be now, while the forces are divided. With that being said, I prowl the property, making sure nothing is out of place.

Several of the carcasses that were left on the main road are missing. None of us bothered to clean anything up, and to be perfectly honest, we were debating about having a barbecue. So a few bodies going missing definitely has piqued my interest.

Walking to the place of the last body, I noticed drag marks where someone or something pulled the body down and around the backside of the general store. Following the blood trail, it leads to the basement where the deliveries are stored. My father is close to me, and I make a motion with my hand, signaling that I need my brother and him with me.

Now that I have backup, it's not as dangerous to go down into the beast's lair. Thankfully for this endeavor, Old Lady Witherspoon, who runs the store, decided to have the stairs replaced this summer. Now they're not as loud and rickety as they used to be. I swear you could hear someone walking down the original stairs from inside the store, no matter who was going up and down them.

At the foot of the stairs, we look around cautiously. The blood trail has thickened here, and the smell of death permeates the interior. Creeping slowly, we get close to the light switch and flick it on, ready for anything. The one thing we weren't ready for was a female Jaguar, leaning over the bodies of the Oxen and eating the raw flesh from their bones.

"Camille, love. Sorry to interrupt your dinner, but you need to dispose of these dogs," a deep, pompous voice sounds from our left, behind the rocks. The female Jaguar leaps into action, heading straight for us. Thankfully, my brother and I are prepared for surprise attacks, and we pull our Bowie knives from the scabbards on our hips. As much as losing a female damages the population, one hell-bent on trying to kill me is not safe to leave living.

Bruiser and I drive our blades up in her chest as her cat wraps its paws around the backs of both of our necks. She leans her head in and bites my shoulder, sinking her teeth deep into my flesh. The crunching of bone almost distracts me from twisting the blade in her chest. Thankfully, my brother only has claws sunk into his shoulder, and he's quick to finish dispatching the female.

"Tsk, tsk, gentlemen. It's very inappropriate for Alphas to run around killing females indiscriminately." His pompous tone grates on my nerves as we try to see exactly where he's hiding. Scanning the storeroom, there are only a few places for him to remain out of sight.

"I wouldn't exactly call you a gentleman when you send your female in to do your dirty work. What happened? Did somebody neuter you or did you just not grow a set?" I ask, attempting to laugh but still holding on to my bleeding shoulder and waiting for my accelerated shifter healing to kick in. Quickly, I glance at my shoulder, and the holes seem to be closing slowly. Hopefully, before this asshole decides to make his move, I'll be healed enough to fight.

A booming laugh echoes in the area from behind the one set of shelving. "Why would I want to get my hands dirty when I can send somebody else to do it for me? Why own a weapon if you will not use it?" he says as he finally steps out into the light. He's dressed oddly in a well-tailored suit and tie. I can tell the suit is expensive by the way the seams are held together.

He's not a species I'm familiar with, but his attitude and the way he carries himself make it clear he's an Alpha. "So you consider females to be tools? Things to be cast aside or traded like they're nothing?" Shaking my head, I watch my brother and father spread out a little further, none of us taking our eyes off this new male.

"Those of us in the Blood Moon pack, a part of the Legion of Vidar, do not tolerate females being abused or mistreated." I reach into my back pocket and pull out the coin Leviathan has given to all his Alphas.

Holding the coin out in front of me with my good arm, I smile. My brother has his cell phone out, no doubt, to connect to the big guy himself. "I, Tyson, Alpha of the Blood Moon pack, president of the Montana chapter of the Legion of Vidar, hereby sentence you to death." I put the coin back in my pocket and glance over at my brother, who nods, letting me know Leviathan agrees. "No longer shall you harm or hunt any females on my watch." I put the force and power of my Alpha status behind my tone. My father and brother waver slightly and take a step back at the force of my Alpha power.

The male laughs, and it's one of those laughs that makes chills run up your spine. Apparently, he knows something we don't. From the phone in my brother's hand, I hear a voice say, "Inbound," before the call disconnects. My brother's eyes widen as he looks between the phone and me. With a jerk of my head, I know we need to leave now. Grabbing hold of my father's jacket, I drag him toward the stairs, and he takes the hint easily.

We barely escape the basement before a great bellowing roar can be heard from downstairs. The floorboards are ripped up, and the building collapses on itself from whatever that male downstairs is doing. The fact that Leviathan is "inbound" scares the living hell out of me. What could be so bad that the founder of the Legion of Vidar, himself, is crawling out of whatever hole it is where he lives to handle this threat?

I DON'T KNOW what's going on down the mountain, but whatever it is, it sounds like something has risen from *Jurassic Park* or maybe a monster from one of those Japanese monster movies from the seventies or eighties that used to be so popular. Even worse than either of those possibilities, it seems something has risen from hell itself and come to scorch the earth. The hair stands up on the back of my neck as we stare down the mountain, watching the general store cave in on itself, falling away to literally nothing.

Titan and Leo gather up the Lionesses after we fish Murphy out of the hole. We head back down toward the town, avoiding the fallen bodies and frozen blood. The next thing we see is Trigger, Bruiser, and their father running at top speed in their human form, yelling for everybody to get back and to get away. It's strange to see three Alphas running and flailing their arms like that.

I've never known Alphas to run from anything, so this new situation definitely concerns me. Titan and Leo move to the edge of the woods at the base of the mountain and grab the clothes they'd left there earlier. After they shift back to their human forms, they head over to meet up with the Wolves.

As fast as I am, I try to catch up with the boys before they stop talking about what's going on instead of letting them hide it from me. But as usual, I'm too late. They keep quiet, and I remain in the dark, not knowing whether we're safe. I head over to where one female told me there's a storage bin full of clothing.

Before I even have the chance to pop the lid on the clothing bin, that dreadful roar sounds again, and this time the head of a hideous-looking monster surfaces from out of the wreckage. I don't know exactly what it is. It looks like a Dragon, but then again, it looks like a Snake on steroids. Whatever it is, I want nothing to do with it.

Staring at this reptilian monster, my heart thunders in my chest. It kind of reminds me of a Hydra but without the multiple heads. The thing roars furiously several more times, all while striking down on the surrounding buildings with its big, blunt nose.

The Wolves recoil, helplessly unable to stop their town from being destroyed. I quickly move and stand behind Leo, wrapping my arms around his taut waist, peeking around the side of his arm. My father, Titan, moves behind me and strokes my hair, trying to comfort me as we stare helplessly at this giant snake creature. I'm afraid to move from my hiding place behind my mate, watching this monster wreak devastation and wipe out the surrounding structures and homes. I see Trigger, standing shoulder to shoulder with his father and brother, at the tree line. They're flanked by his mother and the rest of the pack. As a group, the entire pack watches the destruction of the village many have called home their entire lives.

A second, yet different and more ferocious roar sounds, shaking the earth beneath our feet, and I cower, burrowing myself further under Leo's arm. Bizarrely, Trigger turns and beams a maniacal smile. It's as if he knows something truly terrible is about to happen, but he's happy about it.

"Watch the skies," Trigger says and turns his gaze to look up over the trees. I hear a "whoosh, whoosh," which sounds like giant wings flapping in the air. It's nearly deafening. Trigger gently pulls me free from Leo's grip and moves me closer to an old oak tree, holding me firmly to his chest. "This is about to get very interesting. The big guy has emerged, and he's furious."

Furrowing my brows, I don't bother asking who the "big guy" is. Obviously, he's the one who owns the wings causing the major downdraft. The sky darkens, and it's as if night has fallen when the sound of the beating wings is right over us.

Looking up, I see a gigantic, winged beast with thick black-and-red scales. It's as if a giant, living, armored fortress is flying overhead. I glance over, looking at my other mates, the Wolves, and Titan's pride. Everyone is cowering except the males from the motorcycle club. "Is that your boss? The one who sent you to rescue us?" I ask, trembling in my mate's arms and watching this behemoth go to war.

"Yes," Trigger says, holding me tightly. I've heard the legend of the last great Wyrm Dragon living here in North America. The story is that he protects Omegas because of his unconditional dedication to his true love, the Omega Celeste. The Dragon comes to a stop in the air with his enormous wings beating to keep him airborne. He rears back and rains fire down on the snake creature, burning him to ash in a matter of seconds. My guess is that this monster was an enemy he's been hunting for quite some time.

There was no mercy given and no need for words. The snake's enterprise of abducting and selling Omegas, both male and female alike, has finally been punished. The great Dragon doesn't even bother to land, nor does he acknowledge us standing off to the side. He merely turns and heads back in the exact direction from which he came, leaving a molten pile of rock, charred flesh, and ash in his wake.

Not long after the Dragon leaves, Trigger's phone rings. I hear a soft female voice on the other end, and then my mate confirms the Dragon has left. I overhear that the Dragon's name is Leviathan, which is completely apropos. He is truly a leviathan from the deep, the boogeyman who stalks the night and frightens little children into being good. A creature of legend.

The female on the phone instructs Trigger to send the bill for the repairs to the town directly to Leviathan. That this man, this wonderful, terrifying being, will cover all the costs of repairs. She also informs Trigger that travel will be arranged for the rescued Omegas to return to their people, wherever they were taken from.

The phone call cuts off without so much as a goodbye, and Trigger smiles, looking down at me. "Well, I guess tomorrow, we'll need to go figure out how many homes and buildings will need to be rebuilt and calculate what it's going to cost the big guy to fix everything," he says to his father.

His father shakes his head. "Your mother has wanted some upgrades for the town for a while. I suppose now is as good a time as any to get them done," he says on a chuckle. The disparity between what he says versus the look of heartache on his face makes sense. It's heartbreaking to have your home destroyed before your eyes, but the promise of having it rebuilt should hopefully take some of the weight off his father's shoulders.

CHAPTER TWENTY-ONE

CLAWS

I'M STILL SHOCKED that Leviathan personally came to destroy the snake creature. It definitely wasn't a Basilisk, nor was it a Naga. We'll probably never know what the hell that thing truly was, besides evil. I guess some things are just not meant to be known. His charred remains still smolder in the pit of what was once the general store. I feel horrible for the owner, having lost everything because that hideous monster decided to shift in their basement.

Watching Fiona interact with Trigger and his father in her loving and supportive way warms my heart. She knows full well the Wolves may have numbers, but they can't protect her the way the Lions can. In some sense, I guess it gives me job security as her mate.

And in another sense, I'm concerned because Trigger's father hinted at wanting to retire. And when an Alpha retires, usually his eldest son takes over the pack as the

Alpha. I'm not 100 percent sure, though, whether Trigger is ready to settle down to pack life. He loves the freedom the MC gives him. He can come and go as he pleases, get lost on a long road trip, and have zero responsibilities except to his brothers.

I find myself always watching Fiona, instinctively making sure all her needs are met. She moves from Trigger over to Clutch and snuggles into the big Bruin's side. He's gotten into the habit of laughing, picking her up, and spinning her around. The musical quality of her laughter makes me smile more than I have in a long time. My mother once told me an Omega, even though physically weaker than an Alpha, has a tremendous amount of power when it comes to the pride. The Omega can help a pride grow more tightly connected and stronger or they can destroy a pride, just as an Alpha can.

Glancing around the pack property and the resources it holds, I realize this wouldn't be such a terrible place to live if Trigger decides to assume the role of Alpha of his pack. Trigger's younger brother, Bruiser, can undoubtedly take over Trigger's role as president of the club. He can also easily find replacements for the four of us and have his pick of rooms for his ole lady and him.

The five of us can live here, taking care of our beautiful Fiona. She'd definitely have a better nest here than what we can provide for her in the clubhouse. And it's not like we can't join up with the boys and go for a ride periodically as long as no kittens are involved. My thoughts of the future warms my soul, and my purr rumbles. At the thought of my mate swollen with my cub and my kitten frolicking in the grass, I know I'm grinning like a lovesick fool.

Laughing, Titan slaps his hand on my back. "What's made you so content, son? A feisty little Snow Leopard perhaps?" He motions with his head in the direction of Fiona walking with Clutch.

"Yeah, my happiness is definitely all her fault. Silly female, getting me to settle down." I'm smiling and half laughing between purrs, showing that the change is welcome.

"I can't think of a better, more trustworthy male for Fiona to have ended up with. Now I have to get used to having Wolves, Bears, and that Wolverine thing around." Titan flicks his hand dismissively toward Murphy. "But as long as Fiona is happy, I can tolerate anything. Even that weird smelly little male," Titan says, chuckling.

Part of me understands where he's coming from when it comes to having our Beta in the mate bond. It's not like he could protect her in the cavern with his small animal form. Except for being a fantastic cook, he offers nothing besides his heart and companionship. But somehow, I think heart and companionship are things that truly matter to Fiona.

Still, my Alpha mind finds that bond strange. I can rationalize Clutch being her mate because of the size of his

Bear and the raw power he has. I can also understand Trigger because Wolves are cunning, fast, and excellent hunters. As for myself, even though male Lions generally don't do the bulk of the hunting, we can help provide protection and assist with the hunts. Unlike our wild counterparts, we're involved in the day-to-day business of the pride and providing for the family unit. Speaking of which, I just had a grand idea.

"Hey, boys! How about we go for a hunt for some fresh meat and have a barbecue to celebrate the recovery of the Omegas?" I scan the crowd, looking at everyone gathered, and they all start to cheer.

Not only would a barbeque be a great way to celebrate the rescue of the Omegas, it would also bolster the mental and emotional well-being of the Wolves who just lost their homes due to whatever that snake thing was. Trigger and his father organize their best hunters as does Titan with his pride. Between the Lions and the Wolves, not much will be able to escape the hunt.

Someone in the eighties wrote a song about being "hungry like a Wolf," and they weren't joking. When Wolves are hungry, they're probably the best hunters. There's also that old adage about a hungry Wolf hunting best.

With no warning, they take off, stripping, shifting, and running into the woods. Casually, I stroll over to Fiona and wrap my arms around her, drawing her to my chest.

I lightly press a kiss to her temple and start purring softly, only for her.

"What's put you in such a good mood, Leo?" Fiona's breathy tone makes me smile even more as I lean down and nibble on her jaw, down her neck, and over to her shoulder.

"Besides knowing that you're safe now? Having forever with you?" Between every question, I'm planting a kiss along her shoulder and up her neck. "Besides being the luckiest man alive who's able to hold his mate in his arms?" I punctuate my last question by spinning her around, bending her back, and pressing my lips firmly to hers. I'm putting every ounce of love and affection I have for her into this single kiss.

Fiona's soft purr erupts, answering my own and making my heart swell. I feel her love for me, not only through the bond, but also through her actions. This sweet little creature allowing me to be her mate and her Alpha is one of the greatest gifts she could ever give me.

When we finally break apart, there are brilliant smiles plastered on our faces. Taking her hand, I gently lead her back into town to the place where the pack usually has their big dinners. We find Murphy and Clutch already getting the barbecue pit prepared for when everyone else returns with their kills.

Fiona and I spend the rest of the afternoon helping the others set up. Trigger's mom decides at some point to steal my mate and drag her into the kitchen with her. That just leaves the boys and me to finish getting everything ready for when the others return. As the guys and I work, I see Fiona looking out the kitchen window, watching us. When I catch her eye, I wave at her and then turn back to what I'm doing.

LEVIATHAN COMING in to take care of the snake creature was epic. I've never seen our founder before, and it was definitely something I'll never forget. Fiona is clinging to Claws as the others take off to hunt for tonight's dinner. Murphy and I begin setting up for the barbeque and preparing the pit for the meat we'll soon have to cook. Food is one thing that has always brought the MC together, no matter how tough our mission was.

We set several spits up and organize the spices on the table for the others to pick what flavors they want with their dinners. In one sense, I'm jealous of those who can run fast and hunt. But to be perfectly honest, I prefer my brute strength over speed. I'm happy with who I am and wouldn't change it for the world. Fiona loves me for me, and that's what's important.

Murphy recounts what happened inside the cavern for me after the Crocs found their way in. Shaking my head,

I'm angry at myself for not thinking to look for a second entrance into the cavern. Eventually, Trigger's mom and Fiona come out, carrying trays of appetizers. Claws and I move to take everything from the girls and send Murphy back into the house to help carry whatever is left.

"Clutch, I just wanted to say thank you for protecting Fiona the way you did. The hole in the mountainside was a brilliant idea," Claws says as he picks at the food on the tray closest to him.

Shaking my head, I finish chewing on a chicken finger, then sigh. "Would have been better if I knew about the vent hole at the top." I motion dismissively at the mountain. I'm more disappointed in myself than anything at this point.

"Even Trigger and his dad were unaware of the existence of that cavern. That was quick thinking, sticking Fiona and Murphy in there." He pats my shoulder as he shoves a stuffed pepper into his mouth. "Even with the Crocs finding their way into the cave, Fiona and Murphy were much safer in there than on the side of the mountain," Claws says before walking over to the fire pit and tossing in more wood.

I sit down on the end of the bench, watching the flames flickering under the spit. So many things could have gone wrong today. Thankfully, we mostly came out in one piece. Things can easily be replaced, buildings and towns rebuilt. But lives lost are gone forever. Thinking about this town reminds me of the stories of what happened to my parents' hometown in Siberia before I was born. An avalanche crashed into it in the middle of the night, and only the Bear shifters survived. Hundreds of lives were lost, all because a mining company wanted to make a quick buck.

I snap out of my dark thoughts to find my beautiful mate waving a honeycomb in front of my face, trying to get my attention. "Where did you go just now?" Her soft tone pulls at my heart. My normally sassy mate looks worried about me.

"Just remembering a story my father told me as a cub about how greed wiped out an entire town." I force a smile and pull her flush against my chest, kissing her softly. "It was long before I was born, in a land across the ocean and the coldest place on earth." Fiona's eyebrows rose almost to her hairline.

"Well, okay. As long as my teddy bear is okay, that's all that matters." She punctuates the sentence with a kiss on my nose, then giggles at me. I guess the confused face I'm making over being called a teddy bear is funny to her.

"Teddy bear? Really, Fi? Should I call you kitty or kitten?" I playfully tap her on the nose and smile, waiting for that sass of hers to fire back at me.

"Aw, teddy bear. You can call me anything you want." She pours on a fake southern drawl, enunciating each word. "Just don't call me late for bed. No one likes missin' out on getting' a little lovin'." She kisses my nose, leaving me speechless. She hands me the honeycomb then slowly licks her fingers in front of me.

Seriously, what am I supposed to say to a line like that? She puts a little extra sway into her steps, accentuating that perfect apple bottom of hers. I know now why rappers love writing about a woman's ass. That thing is a piece of art, perfection in motion. Murphy is laughing his ass off at me, and I throw a biscuit at his head.

The little bastard catches the biscuit and takes a bite out of it. "Thanks, man! Just what I needed to take the edge off my hunger." He eats the biscuit and stokes the fire, trying to produce enough coals for when the others return.

I shift my gaze around the pack lands, looking at the destruction that creature caused. Shaking my head, I stand up and move to where some of the older males are huddled. Apparently, there are machines trapped in the one barn that collapsed, and they need them to clear the town. Thankfully for me, my Bear's strength stays with me even when I'm human, so I volunteer to help get the machines out. Claws eventually catches up to me and assists with debris removal. It takes almost an hour to free the excavator. Once it's free, the owner hops in the driver's seat and uses it to free the other machine.

Claws and I stand back in silence, watching how resilient the Wolves are in the face of adversity. The old saying of taking the lemons and making lemonade is something put into practice here. We jump in to help wherever the

Wolves need it, but for the most part, they've got a pretty good handle on things.

The hunting parties return with several deer and some small game. It's an exciting time, seeing everyone's happiness at their successful hunt, then watching the females taking over and sending their mates to go rest. Fiona is busy with Trigger's mom, passing out cold beverages or grabbing things from the house. I decide, instead of being a bump on the proverbial log, I'll help with the cooking and seasoning of the meat.

There's nothing like slowly roasting your dinner over an open fire to make you appreciate the little things in life. Fiona moves between Murphy and me as we handle the two pits, cooking dinner for everyone. Claws joins us and begins slicing the meat off the skewers and placing the first plate on the serving table. The pack, pride, and club take turns filling their plates while the rest of us work on keeping the food coming.

Fiona spends time bouncing between Murphy and me, bringing us drinks and snacks as we cook. How in the nine hells did I ever get so lucky to have such a thoughtful female? I sit back, watching the pack and the MC interacting, and the thought of settling here becomes more appealing.

I'm drawn to this place with the nearby mountains, a good hunting range, as well as a pleasant stream flowing through the center of the property where I can fish. For the most part, Trigger's house remains standing in one piece except the garage which took a hit. I sit back, listening to the Alpha of the pack talking to his people, discussing the future and how they plan to proceed from here with the recovery. All his plans seem solid enough to work out just fine for everyone involved.

CHAPTER TWENTY-THREE
TRIGGER

I RECOGNIZE that look my father has as he looks around the pack and then stares at me for several seconds. He's been contemplating the future for the last several months, trying to decide when the best possible time would be for him to step down as Alpha.

Traditionally, it's usually a fight to the death for the new Alpha to ascend and take over a pack. Thankfully, we're long past those violent customs of years gone by, and now, there's just a succession of power. To be perfectly honest, I'd rather have my father at my side to guide me through the first year.

What I'm most thankful for is the support system I have within my motorcycle club. If Dad chooses now to step down, I'll ask my brother, Bruiser, to step up as the president of our chapter. That way, there are two successions of power and two people left standing to assist with the day-to-day tasks until the new leader is comfortable with his position.

I'm just not sure how Clutch, Claws, Murphy, and Fiona would feel about living on pack lands or with me becoming Alpha so my father can finally retire. It's one of those discussions I've dreaded having with even my motorcycle club. Now, I have to worry about having the discussion with my mate and her three other mates as well.

The conversation between Fiona and me won't be that difficult. I'm concerned about speaking to Clutch and Claws since both of them are Alphas in their own right. I don't know how they'd feel about me being deemed the dominant Alpha because of my position in the pack.

Dread fills my stomach as my father walks over toward our small group, and I have a bad feeling I know exactly what he's about to say.

"Son, with all things considered and the actions of you and your brothers, I think it's time for a transition of power," my father's voice booms and draws the attention of the entire pack. I am—and at the same time, I'm not—shocked that this became a topic of conversation today. Especially after how we successfully handled keeping the pack safe in a time of extreme danger.

"Father, please allow me a few moments to speak with my family, and I'll give you an answer in a few moments," I say as respectfully as possible, still acknowledging my father not only as my dad but also as the leader of the pack. With a terse nod of his head, he backs away and walks over to where my mother sits.

I stand up and start pacing in front of the table, not knowing how to start this conversation even though Dad already kicked it out into plain sight. So I do the simplest thing possible and put the ball into their court. "What's everyone's thoughts?" Short, sweet, and to the point. I'll wait and watch for everyone's reactions.

Fiona is the first to stop what she's doing, and she looks up at me with a smile. "Settling down in a community would be best if sometime in the future everyone wants little ones. The question, though, is Ty, are you ready to take over the leadership of your father's pack?" My beloved little hellcat really just put everything into perspective.

The crucial question and the one I'd not dared ask myself is whether I'm ready. I bend down and kiss her gently on the forehead, then stand up and smile. "It would honor me to take over the pack of my birth. But it's not just me anymore. I have you and our nest mates to consider. I need to know everyone's feelings on the subject."

Clutch stands up and pulls me into a back-thumping hug, then releases me. "If Fiona thinks this is best for our future, I stand behind our mate. Besides, you have a Bruin and a Lion Alpha at your side, without question. We have your back from now until we draw our last breath." Clutch pulls me in for another quick hug once more before sitting down, earning himself a kiss from Fiona.

I glance over at Claws and wait for his decision. He doesn't stand. Instead, he tilts his head to the side and smiles up at me. "We are what's best for this pack's future. Yes, the open road is fun and being thrown into danger at least once a month by Leviathan definitely keeps the blood pumping. But speaking honestly, we're not getting younger, and it's about damn time we settle down." His eyes flare golden yellow with the power of his Lion behind it. That's three votes for me to assume the mantle of Alpha in the pack.

Last, I look over at our little Beta, Murphy, who just shakes his head, laughing. "I got nothing, boss. The two Alphas said it best, and to be perfectly honest, I'm not going against either of them or Fiona. They'll skin me." I can't help but laugh at how Murphy has removed himself from the decision-making process. I guess the fear of being eaten, drawn and quartered, or skinned alive is real.

"Well, I guess that solves it," I say as I throw my hands up into the air. I spin around to face where my father is standing, and I see him already laughing. "Hey, pack. There's a new Alpha in town," I yell as I throw my arms wide to the applause and cheers of my childhood pack. My announcement throws the party into full gear. Extra beverages and food are now being pulled out to feed the celebrating masses.

My brother, Bruiser, walks up to me and tilts his head to the side. "So, who's taking over the club?"

I can't help but grin and grab my brother around the back of his neck, pressing my forehead to his. "You are. You're the best choice to keep the club moving in the direction we've been heading for the last fifteen years. I'll advise Leviathan of the succession of power tomorrow. Tonight, let's just enjoy it and relax for once."

Cheers ring up around us again when my announcement that my brother is taking over leadership of the MC is heard by all. It's virtually impossible to be in two places at once, and at least this way, in addition to Titan's pride, my brother will have the full support of our pack. The future, for once, looks certain and bright, especially since a majority of my guys found mates during this last mission. Life simply can't get any better than this.

EPILOGUE – TRIGGER

FIVE YEARS LATER...

Like all good things, eventually some have to end. Before my father's eighty-first year, he's succumbed to old age. In his honor, we erected a monument and a grove to honor those who had fallen during the battle from whatever that snake creature was. We even built a museum with the snake's head as the centerpiece. First-hand descriptions of the events line different walls within the memorial. We documented every square inch of damage the creature caused.

True to his word, Leviathan not only provided financial support, he also sent two teams to work on the property. The demolition team arrived first and ended up clearing out 80 percent of the existing damaged structures. And under Leviathan's command, they erected new buildings and storefronts. He even had the infrastructure of our sewer and water delivery systems upgraded to the most current technology available.

In his infinite wisdom, he added a doctor's office, a clinic, and a small triage hospital to handle any birthing complications the females in the pack might possibly have. Per my suggestion, two schools were built as well as a free public library. I wanted to stress the need for continuing education, so if any of my people look outside our borders for either their mate or for work, we've educated them enough to provide for themselves and their future families.

Leviathan seemed pleased with the amount of forethought I put into the construction project. I was running on the theory that if he was offering to upgrade our lives and make the place better for us and future generations, I'd take full advantage of the opportunity. After all, it would be foolish of me if I didn't try to better the lives of my people and my family.

Like all new families, we've had our difficulties, trials, and tribulations, day in and day out. As much as we hope and plan for our family in the future, at this moment, it's not a priority. We need to make sure the pack and those living with the pack are living their best lives.

Fiona came up with a five-year plan for us. In that plan, at some point, she'd like to try for a family. Given the issues her people have in reproducing, we know it might come down to us adopting children. We had that discussion just the other night, although Fiona was afraid to have it with us. We did our best to comfort her through the tears, the upset, the fear, and the frustration she was dealing with.

The one thing that we all agreed on was that as long as she loves us, we're happy and we need nothing else. What Fiona doesn't know is that we're having a Big Brother and Big Sister event here this summer. Every child coming here is looking for their forever home. If it's Fiona's desire to adopt one or a half dozen of them, the guys and I will support her decision 1000 percent.

Fiona's plan for the pack's growth is as solid as I'd expect a seasoned Alpha would be able to create. She's proven herself to be one of the best Lunas the pack has ever seen. She received the title honorarily, even though she's not a Wolf. Her care and concern for all the members of the pack make me very proud of the woman she's become.

Her maternal instinct has provided love and comfort to all the fresh faces we welcome into our borders every year. Currently, as we do for every major solstice, we invite not only Titan's pride, but also the MC to the pack lands to join in on the hunts. It's a great time to watch everyone gather around and work together as a team to bring down the food for the night's banquet.

I look back toward the house and see Fiona standing on the porch, watching over the festivities, making sure everything is going according to plan. Several cubs and pups run around on the deck near her. She's watching them for their parents while they hunt or help set up for everyone else's arrival. I'm surprised she's content to watch other people's children rather than attempting to have children of her own.

She takes her job as Luna seriously and is constantly all over town, checking on the inhabitants. Even after everything was said and done, we're still constantly finding little things that need to be mended or replaced from the battle with the snake. Some of the damage was hidden deep within some buildings, while others were patently visible at the time of the attack. I guess things will never be completely healed. But through the hard work and dedication of all the pack members, as well as everyone within the MC, we've managed to pull everything back together as close as possible to the way it was if not better.

There was nothing more exciting than the ribbon-cutting that happened almost a year after the attack. A representative from The Hangman showed up and presented a gift to the town from Leviathan and himself. So now, in our town center, a statue of Leviathan's Dragon burning the snake to ash is proudly displayed where everyone can see it. I'm guessing it's his not so subtle reminder of what he did for us, and therefore, that he deserves our unfettered loyalty.

On the flip side, my brother has expanded the MC to over thirty members, including some Lions from Titan's pride. He is now the leader of one of the most diverse MCs in the state.

Off in the distance, we hear the rumble of the MC's motorcycles as they approach the town. I see my brother and his men heading straight toward the picnic area. It's nice to have my brother still close, yet far enough away that he's not up my ass.

As the guys arrive, the children line the road, excited to see the motorcycles roll into town. The children cheer and wave at each biker as they rumble by. Hearing the deep purr of the bikes makes me miss the days when I roamed the world, wild and free. But just as I get lost in my memories, Fiona wraps her arms around me and brings me back to the present. All things considered, I wouldn't change my life for anything. I love my mate, and we've formed a tight-knit family unit here with the guys.

Fiona grabs my hand and leads me back to where everyone else is gathered for dinner. The banquet is far more than I'd expected. The summer solstice is upon us, and the announcements of the babies born is the highlight of the afternoon. Several pregnancies have also been announced, and Fiona starts to nervously tap dance around, looking more and more uncomfortable as the evening progresses. Titan is the first to pull his daughter to him in concern. I can tell the moment Fiona unloads everything on him because his eyebrows shoot up, and then he looks around.

Taking the hint, Clutch, Claws, and I move over to him to see he's pissed. "Did you know?" Titan's voice booms as he looks between Clutch and me. Arching a brow, I look over at Claws, then back to Titan.

"Why are you asking us and not him?" I motion to Claws, then look at Clutch, who gives me a brief nod.

Growling low in the back of his throat, Titan snarls, curling his upper lip. "Because it's one of you two fuckers who did it!"

Shaking my head, I drop to my knees before Fiona and take her hands. "Baby, please tell me what I did so I can fix it. I'm sorry for whatever I fucked up." I'm not even sure what I'm apologizing for, but it's worth a shot.

Tears stream down Fiona's cheeks, and she rushes forward and buries her face in Clutch's pecs. Shocked and puzzled, I stand up as Claws pulls Fiona from Clutch. He nuzzles her neck and starts purring deeply, trying to settle her nerves. Then his purr begins to sound broken, and he lifts his head suddenly. "Fi? Is it true?" he asks softly in a voice that's barely audible to anyone else.

Fiona gives him the slightest nod, and he picks her up, hugging her, spinning around in a circle, laughing. "This is the best day ever!" he yells, leaving Clutch and me confused.

"What the fuck has gotten into him?" Murphy asks, walking to us and staring at Claws like he's completely lost his fucking mind.

Shaking my head, I step closer to a laughing Claws. "Mind sharing with the rest of the class?" I tilt my head to the side, looking at him curiously.

He laughs even harder. "One of you two assholes is going to be a dad." Claws carries our mate away, and I turn and stare at Clutch. The big Bruin turns pale and starts swaying on his feet. I turn my head for just a moment to see where Claws is taking Fiona when I hear a thud behind me. Clutch apparently couldn't handle what Claws said. So what if he called us assholes? Claws calls us that all the time, so it shouldn't come as a surprise to Clutch. I keep walking, replaying the conversation over in my head.

Then it hits me. Quickly, I turn my head and look at Clutch, then to Fiona and Claws. "Holy fuck, I'm going to be a dad . . ."

With every season, there's growth and death. Not every victory is won easily. We'd just about given up on having children of our own. But now, Fiona is carrying what will hopefully be our rainbow cub. Only time will tell, but Goddess willing, this time will be it—the beginning of our new adventure.

Join my Newsletter for updates: Newsletter Signup

Join my readers group for contests and giveaways: Serenity's Den

Also by me: The Aurora Marelup Saga

The Dark Angel Chronicles